Dear Reader,

Looking back over the years, I find it hard to realize that twenty-six of them have gone by since I wrote my first book—*Sister Peters in Amsterdam*. It wasn't until I started writing about her that I found that once I had started writing, nothing was going to make me stop—and at that time I had no intention of sending it to a publisher. It was my daughter who urged me to try my luck.

I shall never forget the thrill of having my first book accepted—a thrill I still get each time a new story is accepted. To me, writing is such a pleasure, and seeing a story unfolding on my old typewriter is like watching a film and wondering how it will end. Happily, of course.

To have so many of my books republished is such a delightful thing to happen and I can only hope that those who read them will share my pleasure in seeing them on the bookshelves again...and enjoy reading them.

Betty Neels

Betty Neels spent her childhood and youth in Devonshire before training as a nurse and midwife. She was an army nursing sister during the war, married a Dutchman and subsequently lived in Holland for fourteen years. She lives with her husband in Dorset, and has a daughter and a grandson. Her hobbies are reading, animals, old buildings and writing. On retirement from nursing Betty started to write, incited by a lady in a library bemoaning the lack of romantic novels.

Mrs. Neels is always delighted to receive fan letters, but would truly appreciate it if they could be directed to Harlequin Mills & Boon Ltd., 18-24 Paradise Road, Richmond, Surrey, TW9 1SR, England.

Books by Betty Neels

HARLEQUIN ROMANCE

JUDITH
MIDNIGHT SUN'S MAGIC
SUN AND CANDLELIGHT
PHILOMENA'S MIRACLE
HANNAH
A MATTER OF CHANCE
WINTER WEDDING
STORMY SPRINGTIME

ENCHANTING SAMANTHA
HEIDELBERG WEDDING
POLLY
TULIPS FOR AUGUSTA
LAST APRIL FAIR
TEMPESTUOUS APRIL
WHEN MAY FOLLOWS
MIDSUMMER STAR

BETTY NEELS

TULIPS FOR AUGUSTA

COLLECTOR'S EDITION

HARLEQUIN®

TORONTO • NEW YORK • LONDON
AMSTERDAM • PARIS • SYDNEY • HAMBURG
STOCKHOLM • ATHENS • TOKYO • MILAN • MADRID
PRAGUE • WARSAW • BUDAPEST • AUCKLAND

ISBN 0-373-63134-0

TULIPS FOR AUGUSTA

First North American Publication 2000.

Copyright © 1971 by Betty Neels.

This edition published by arrangement with Harlequin Books S.A.

® and TM are trademarks of the publisher. Trademarks indicated with ® are registered in the United States Patent and Trademark Office, the Canadian Trade Marks Office and in other countries.

Visit us at www.eHarlequin.com

Printed in U.S.A.

CHAPTER ONE

MISS AUGUSTA BROWN climbed the old-fashioned staircase leading to the Private Patients' Wing, planting her small feet, shod in regulation black lace-ups, with a deliberation which amounted to slow motion. She was seething with temper, disappointment, and a burning sense of injustice, for half an hour previously she had been sent for by Matron, to be told by that somewhat awe-inspiring little lady that she was to go to Private Wing for an unspecified period, until such time as Staff Nurse Bates returned from sick leave. Augusta disliked Bates anyway—a tiresome girl, making the most of a grumbling appendix—and she loathed Private Patients. She had told Matron so, her pleasant voice sharpened by determination; but it had been useless, of course. She had returned to Men's Surgical, where she had been staffing most happily for the year since she had qualified, and told Sister and such of the nurses and patients who happened to be around. She told Archie Dukes too—he had been houseman on the ward for the last six months, and they had become good friends. Now she wouldn't be able to see so much of him; junior house surgeons didn't find their way to PP very often…they would have to rely upon the odd meeting in one of the hospital's innumerable corridors, and trust to luck that they would occasionally be free at the same time; a not very likely chance, for she had often heard Bates grumbling about the number of split duties she

5

had...it was the best way to get work done on PP, because most of the patients had visitors each afternoon, so that any treatment needed was set aside until after tea, when the staff nurse could cope with it when she returned at five o'clock. A fine state of affairs, thought Augusta resentfully, who had been in the habit of sharing alternate duties with Sister.

She reached the top of the stairs, pushed open the swing doors before her, and went, still slowly, into Sister's office.

Sister Cutts was sitting at her desk—a tall, lean woman, who had reached middle age without making any effort to do something about it. Her greying hair was strained back into a scanty bun, her thin face, devoid of lipstick, bore traces of the wrong shade of powder. She had beautiful, dark, melancholy eyes and splendid teeth. Augusta, studying her as she reported for duty, thought for the hundredth time that it was a great pity that no one had taken Sister Cutts in hand...she was an excellent nurse, and treated her staff with an aloof fairness which they found distinctly daunting, and she had no close friends. She looked up as Augusta entered, smiled briefly and said:

'Good morning, Staff Nurse Brown. Sit down, will you? I'll be ready for you in a minute.'

She returned to whatever she was doing and became instantly absorbed in it, leaving Augusta to sit and stare out of the window. PP was on the fourth floor, well away from the noise and bustle of the courtyard below. She watched an ambulance slide rapidly up to the Accident Room entrance, reflecting at the same time, with an uplift of her spirits, that she would be going on holiday in three weeks' time anyway, and probably by the time she got back, Bates

would be on duty again. She interrupted her thoughts
for a moment, to watch while the ambulance men
threw open its door and carefully drew out a stretcher
and bore it away out of sight. She wondered what it
was—not an accident, for the flash wasn't on; she
mulled over the possibilities and then abandoned
them for the more cheerful subject of holidays. She
would go home for a day or so, to the small village
in Dorset where her father was the local vet, and then
she would go over to Holland; to Alkmaar, where her
mother's two elderly aunts lived. It would be quiet
staying with them, but it made a change, and as her
mother often reminded her, it was good for her Dutch.

She looked across the desk at Sister Cutts, but her
head was still bowed over her writing. Augusta fought
a desire to yawn and began some complicated mental
arithmetic to discover if she would have enough
money to buy some new clothes; even if the holiday
was to be a quiet one, there was no need for her to
look a dowd. But her arithmetic was poor, and presently she gave up her sums, and sat staring at her
hands folded tidily upon her white apron. They were
pretty hands, small and finely shaped, with pale pink
nails—her only beauty, her brother Charles had gen-
erously conceded, pointing out with brutal frankness
that with a turned-up nose like hers, and a mouth like
a letterbox and carroty hair to boot, she was no picture. This unpleasing description of her person in no
way distressed Augusta; for one thing, it was grossly
exaggerated. Her hair was indeed a peculiar shade of
pale copper, but it was soft and fine and her nose was
nice enough, even if it did turn up the merest bit at
the end, and as for her mouth, large it might be, but
it was a good shape and curved sweetly at the corners.

She was no beauty, but on the other hand, she wasn't plain—and she had most satisfactory eyes...vividly green, fringed and browed silkily with a deep coppery brown. But she would have liked to have been taller and slimmer—as a child she had been plump, and although the plumpness had melted away, leaving curves in the right places and a slim waist, it was only in the last few years that she had weaned her family from the habit of addressing her as Roly—even now, they occasionally forgot.

Sister Cutts spoke. 'Now, Staff Nurse, if we run through the Kardex together—twenty rooms, as you know—three empty at the moment, but there are two appendices coming in this afternoon under Mr James. I'll start with Room One. There are several patients who are not seriously ill—you appreciate that, of course.'

Augusta made a small sound of agreement. PP always had its quota of patients with mild chest infections, or needing a check-up; for there were still those who could afford the fees to lie in comfort while various tests were carried out, instead of going to Out-Patients and waiting their turn; just as there were those who preferred to come into hospital while they had a course of antibiotics. They were quite entitled to their beds and they paid heavy fees; all the same Augusta felt vaguely sorry for them, for if only they weren't so rich and had jobs, they wouldn't have so much time to worry about themselves.

'Marlene Jones,' said Sister Cutts in a no-nonsense voice. 'T's and A's.'

It took quite a time to go through the Kardex; Augusta listened carefully and then followed Sister out into the corridor which stretched on either side of the

office; the patients' rooms on one side of it; a long
line of windows overlooking a wide vista of chimney
pots, church spires and a distant view of St Paul's,
on the other. Augusta gazed out upon this urban scene
and wondered for the hundredth time why she had
ever come to London in the first place. She had a
sudden longing to be home, in the paddock behind
the house, with the dogs and Bottom, the old pet donkey, and a pleasant smell of baking coming from the
kitchen. She wondered, fleetingly, if Sister Cutts was
considerate about days off... She caught that lady's
eye, and hastily opened the door of Room One.

The occupant was rolling about in the bed, scream-
ing—a small girl of six or thereabouts, very pretty
and quite obviously spoiled. The child's mother was
standing by the bed, looking helpless, but when she
saw them come in, she spoke at once and quite nas-
tily.

'Really, Sister, surely someone...darling Marlene
has such a sore throat...I should have thought that a
nurse...'

'Did you ring, Mrs Jones?' asked Sister Cutts
briskly.

'Well, no...all the same, the nurses should have
heard her crying—or at least come and see Marlene
every few minutes or so.'

Sister Cutts received this observation with faintly
lifted eyebrows.

'There is considerable noise in a hospital, Mrs
Jones—the nurses go about their work, and only stop
what they are doing when a bell is rung, unless the
patient is too ill to ring it, in which case other arrangements are made. In any case, you, Marlene's
mother, are here.'

She went over to the bed without hurry. 'Stop crying, Marlene, for that will make your throat more sore, you know, and then you won't be able to go home—let me see—the day after tomorrow, isn't it?'

Marlene snivelled grumpily, eyeing Sister Cutts with the malevolence of the angry young and a certain amount of respect.

'Ice cream for tea,' remarked Sister. 'This is Staff Nurse Brown who will look after you when I'm not here.'

She turned away, leaving Augusta to go to the bed, where she was studied fixedly before Marlene said, in a voice thickened by tears and soreness, 'You've got green eyes.' And then, 'Do you have ice cream for tea?'

'No such luck,' said Augusta cheerfully. 'I shall come and see you eat yours instead.' She smiled at the red, tear-stained face, smiled again, briefly, at Mrs Jones, and followed Sister Cutts out of the room.

The patient next door was an old man—very old, very ill, and, said Sister, as they closed the door upon him; very rich. His wife was still a young woman— too young, observed Sister, darkly.

The third patient was of more interest, though not from a medical point of view. Miss Dawn Dewey, a film starlet, was suffering from a feverish cold which she referred to, rather grandly, as Coryza; she also talked vaguely about threatened complications. But Augusta, standing primly beside Sister, thought that she looked remarkably healthy...indeed, she found the patient's condition far less interesting than the ruffled and ribboned nightgown she was wearing. She went nearer the bed to greet the young woman in it, and decided that the lace was real...something to tell the girls when she went to dinner. But despite the gorgeous nightie and the quantities of flowers about the room, Miss Dewey looked discontented and a little vapid, although as Augusta reminded herself, the poor dear did have a very nasty cold.

She followed Sister in and out of four or five rooms, saying 'How do you do?' to their occupants and studying them with her bright green eyes. Some of the patients were ill, and her pleasant face softened with sympathy, for she was a soft-hearted girl who hated to see suffering and pain—which was why, of course, she was such a good nurse.

They retraced their steps presently to the other half of the corridor beyond Sister's office, calling first upon a charming middle-aged woman with a pretty, weak face and a gushing manner—a chronic alcoholic, who came in regularly in vain attempts to cure her. Next to her was the Brigadier... Sister had warned Augusta about him, for he was peppery in the extreme, and prone to use Army language if annoyed, and that, it seemed, was often. Augusta rather liked him. But it was the next patient who caught her fancy: Lady Belway, a bad-tempered old lady in a lace nightcap and a marabou cape, who lay in bed with a fractured neck of femur, looking like a chained lioness. She lifted a lorgnette on a gold chain to stare at Augusta as Sister introduced her, and said in a commanding voice:

'She's only a child—far too young to look after me—or anyone else for that matter.'

Augusta, who had great-aunts of her own, allowed herself a faint smile and said nothing, leaving Sister to answer. 'Staff Nurse is a most capable member of our staff, Lady Belway—highly thought of by the consultants.'

Augusta blinked at this generous testimonial, and the old lady grunted. 'How old are you?'

Augusta blinked again with her sable lashes. 'Twenty-three.'

Lady Belway stared rudely at her. 'Extraordinary hair,' she remarked. And before she could say anything more:

'Yes, isn't it?' agreed Augusta coolly, 'but it makes no difference to my nursing, Lady Belway.' She smiled kindly, her eyes twinkling, and after a long second, the old lady smiled back.

'I've a filthy temper,' she observed with complacence, 'but I suppose you're trained to ignore it.'

Augusta considered this remark. 'If you mean do we let that sort of thing upset us—no, we don't, but that doesn't mean we ignore the patients.' She smiled again and followed Sister to the door, and the old lady called after them, 'Come back and talk to me, Nurse Brown,' which command Augusta acknowledged with another non-committal smile, and Sister with the acid remark that Lady Belway was mistaken; Nurse Brown was Staff Nurse Brown...

Back in the office, she said, 'I understand that you are going on holiday in a week or so, Staff Nurse. Until then perhaps you will take over Staff Nurse Bates' off-duty.'

Augusta said 'Yes, Sister,' because she fancied that it wouldn't be of much use saying anything else, and as she took off her cuffs to prepare for work, she thought nostalgically of Men's Surgical, where Sister, who wasn't a great deal older than herself, had the pleasing habit of offering her a choice of days off, and lent an understanding ear when Augusta had a date with Archie.

She was about to go to her dinner, when Sister Cutts passed the remark that she would be taking a half day, and she was sure that Augusta would manage very well. One of the part-time staff nurses would take over for the afternoon, and Augusta would be good enough to come back on duty at five o'clock. Over dinner, Augusta unburdened herself to those particular staff nurses who were her friends, and then in company with two of them who had half days, took herself out for a little window-shopping, followed by a recklessly extravagant tea at Fortnum and Mason's. She arrived back on duty with a bare minute to spare to take the report from the part-time staff nurse, a large placid girl with a husband and two small children to look after. Augusta, still a little breathless from her hurrying, envied her her unshakable calm.

The evening went better than she had expected— she had three nurses on with her, so that she was able to leave most of the treatments to the more senior of them, leaving her free to deal with doctor's visits, Matron's report and suppers. Suppers were tricky. The trays looked tempting, and Augusta, who was hungry, could have eaten the delicate little dishes of chicken or fish with relish; but several of the patients felt otherwise. She did the after-supper round, trying not to feel irritated at the petty complaints about the wrong kind of sauce and not enough salt. Only the ill patients, she noticed, thanked her without complaint.

Lady Belway, glaring at her from her high stacked pillows, delivered a pithy diatribe on hospital food and her own supper in particular, while Augusta stood patiently. Presently she paused for breath, and when

Augusta still said nothing, asked, 'Well, haven't you anything to say?'

Augusta considered, in no way disconcerted by the old lady's fierce tongue. 'I think the least said the better, don't you, Lady Belway?' she asked at length. 'And now, how about an egg-nog with a hint of brandy, since you didn't enjoy your supper.'

Lady Belway gave a snort of laughter. 'You're no fool, gal—but of course, you wouldn't be with those eyes. Yes, I'll have your egg-nog—if it's drinkable.'

It was an hour or so later, in that quiet, brief doldrum of time between the nurses going to supper and the night staff coming on duty, that Augusta, her report written, discovered that Lady Belway's TPR hadn't been recorded in the day book…she might as well do it now. She went unhurriedly along the corridor, tapped on the door and went in. Lady Belway had visitors—two of them: a girl, a gorgeous girl with dark hair and eyes, and wearing, Augusta noted with a sharp female eye, equally gorgeous clothes. The second visitor was a man, sitting on one of the flimsy cane chairs the hospital provided for its visitors' comfort. It creaked horribly as he got up, which didn't surprise her in the least, for he was well over six foot tall and a large man, with a massive chest and shoulders under his well tailored jacket. She would have liked to have had a good look at him, but she had come for a chart, not to stare at strange men. She said pleasantly, 'I'm sorry, Lady Belway, I didn't know that you had visitors. I need your chart.'

She had unhooked it from the end of the bed as she spoke, and was already making for the door, having cast an all-enveloping smile at its occupants. The man was there first; his large hand closed on the door

handle just as she had extended hers...only he didn't
open the door. After an awkward moment, she
glanced up to look into pale blue eyes that twinkled
rather nicely. He was, she saw, good-looking, with
straw-coloured hair brushed smoothly back from a
wide forehead, a commanding nose and a well-
shaped, firm mouth. The mouth was smiling now—a
small half mocking smile. He said softly in a deep
voice, 'My godmother's quite right; you don't look
old enough.'

Augusta's mouth opened, showing little white
teeth; for a moment she looked as though she was
going to grind them. Instead she shut her mouth again
while she gave him a long, cool glance before saying
finally with dignity, 'I'm glad your fears are groundless,' and when he opened the door, swept through,
her carroty head high. At least a satisfactory exit, she
thought, ruffled, and found him beside her in the corridor.

She started to walk away from him, but he put out
a hand and caught her lightly by the arm. She didn't
move; she had had enough schoolroom fights with her
brother when they were children to know when it was
to her advantage to keep still.

'That's better—I only want to know something
about Lady Belway, and you were so intent on flounc-
ing off before I had a chance to open my mouth.'

She went a little pink, because she hadn't thought
that at all, and he went on, as though he had read her
thoughts, 'Did you think that I was going to make a
pass at you? My dear Staff Nurse, I don't like carroty
hair.'

At this outrageous remark the pink turned to scarlet. Goaded, she snapped, 'I'm not such a desperate

old maid that I welcome—or expect—a pass from a man like you!' Which remark didn't help in the least, as he laughed with genuine amusement, and then asked in quite a different voice—placid yet authoritative, 'My godmother—she isn't very happy here. Oh, I know that she has every attention and kindness, but I wondered if she could be got home soon, if we could find a nurse.'

Augusta fixed her eyes on the fine grey suiting of his jacket. She said stiffly, 'I can't tell you that. I'm temporary here and didn't come until today; in any case, I think you should see Sister Cutts or Mr Weller-Pratt.' She glanced up and wondered why he smiled as though he was amused at something. 'He's the orthopaedic surgeon in charge of Lady Belway's case,' she explained carefully. 'If you care to telephone him or Sister—' She stopped. The sound of quiet feet on the stairs meant the night staff. Before she could speak, he said easily, 'Thanks. I won't keep you—the night staff are coming and you will want to give the report. Goodnight.'

He went back into Lady Belway's room again, leaving her to hurry to the office. The two night nurses were already there—a junior and a staff nurse, a close friend of Augusta's who said at once:

'Gussie, who was that? That handsome giant you were dallying with in the corridor? I hope he stays until I can get on the round.'

Augusta sat down and the other two drew up chairs—something they wouldn't have dared to do if Sister had been on duty; however...

'I don't know who he is,' said Augusta shortly, 'and I don't care.' She was still smarting under his remark about her hair. 'He's visiting Lady Belway and there's a girl with him—wearing a trouser suit.' She described it at some length and rather enviously. Trouser suits looked marvellous on elegant beanpoles, which she was not. She sighed and said uselessly, 'Oh, well!' and flipped the Kardex open and began. 'Marlene Jones, T's and A's—second day...'

During her complicated walk through the hospital to the Nurses' Home she wondered briefly how it was that Lady Belway's visitor had known about her giving the report to the night nurses. In general, visitors hadn't a clue as to how the hospital kept its wheels turning...either he was a very observant man and had been a frequent visitor, or he knew something about hospitals. She considered this unlikely, his appearance had struck her forcibly as that of a member of the leisured class, and he had the assurance and easy manner of those born with the silver spoon. Her brows drew together in a heavy frown, so that when she joined her closer friends in the sitting room there was a general chorused question as to whether she had had a beastly day. Presently, soothed by strong tea and sympathy, she went away to have a bath, and came back, dressing-gowned and ready for bed, to join the others, similarly attired, in watching a spine-chilling film on TV. It was sufficiently horrific to allow her to forget all about the man who didn't like carroty hair.

She remembered him the next morning, though, and over a brisk cup of coffee she was bidden to drink with Sister, mentioned him, hoping that she would hear who he was: her hopes were dashed. Sister observed:

'I've never heard of him. If he wishes to see me he has only to come to the office when I am here, or if he prefers, he can make an appointment with Mr Weller-Pratt.' She dismissed him, to Augusta's disappointment, in favour of the day's work. 'I shall want you to go to Theatre with Miss Toms—she is highly strung and has a low threshold to pain.'

Augusta groaned inwardly. Miss Toms' sensitive feelings would make even the management of a simple operation to remove her appendix a misery for herself as well as the nurses. Presently, obedient to Sister's wishes, she escorted Miss Toms down to the anaesthetic room and held her frantic, restless hand in a reassuring grip and talked to her in a soft, gentle voice that slowly but surely doused poor Miss Toms' terror. She was coming back through the theatre wing's swing door, pinning her cap as she went when she met Lady Belway's visitor again. His 'Hullo' was easy and wholly without surprise. She was trying to think of something to say when he fell into step beside her, remarking, 'Busy, I see…somehow you don't strike me as the type to enjoy Private Wing.'

She had started to say 'I h…' when she remembered that he was hardly someone in whom she could confide her true feelings regarding Private Wing. She closed her pretty mouth firmly and continued to walk sedately towards the stairs. It was at this moment that she saw Archie coming towards them, and was still deciding if she should stop and speak to him or walk on when he drew level with them and said, as though she were alone:

'Hullo, Gussie. See you this evening—same place,' and was on his way again.

Fortunately, they had reached the stairs—Augusta was going up, and she hoped devotedly that her companion was going down. He was, but before he went

he said in what she considered to be a hatefully
smooth voice:

'What a relief!' She had turned on her heel, but
with a fatal curiosity, paused to ask why, to be told,
'I was beginning to think that you didn't like men.
Of course it's a blow to my ego that you don't like
me, but that is something which can be dealt with
later.'

Augusta told herself that she hadn't the least idea
of what he was talking about. She stared at him, her
eyes bright green saucers. She said primly, 'Goodbye'
and flew upstairs two at a time in a whirl of starched
skirts, ashamed that instead of thinking about her evening out with Archie she was wholly concerned with
the tall stranger. Not, she told herself stoutly, that she
found him in the least attractive—indeed, he was rude
and arrogant. She told herself this twice, because it
didn't ring quite true. She wondered how he behaved
towards someone he liked—that lovely dark girl, for
instance. He had a delightful voice—she frowned a
little, because now she came to think about it, he had
an accent—a very faint accent which tugged, elusive
as smoke, at the edge of her senses.

She slipped through the door to PP and forgot him
instantly in the hurry and exactitude of her work, and
when his image persisted in its invasion of her mind
during the rest of the day, she very sensibly ignored
it. But that evening, on the way home from the cinema with Archie, she was reminded of him once more
by her companion, who wanted to know, without
much interest, who he was and what she had been
doing with him anyway. She explained, and when Archie remarked that he had got the impression that her
companion had appeared a high-handed fellow,

agreed with him cheerfully, adding the rider that probably he was married or engaged to the girl he had been with in Lady Belway's room—or at any rate, very close friends. Strangely, she didn't fancy the idea, until she remembered how he had said, very plainly indeed, that he didn't like carroty hair. She said, apropos of nothing at all:

'What colour would you call my hair, Archie?'

He gave her an astonished look. 'Good lord, what on earth do you want to know for? I suppose it's…' he paused. 'Coppery?' he queried cautiously, and was relieved when she smiled.

'I'm going on holiday in a couple of weeks,' she remarked, as they waited for the bus to take them back to St Jude's. 'You'll have to find yourself another girl to take out.' And she was not altogether pleased when he said carelessly, 'Oh, that'll be easy enough.' She wasn't even faintly in love with him, but she had liked to think that he was at least a little in love with her, even if it was only temporary. Apparently not.

Later, in bed thinking about it, she had to admit that Archie was a dear, but if she were in his shoes, she'd take jolly good care not to fall in love with a nurse when there was still at least two years' postgraduate course to get through. It was lucky she hadn't fallen in love with him. She had, like any other girl of twenty-three, fancied herself in love several times, but never to touch her heart, and never for more than a few weeks at a time. To her annoyance, she found herself thinking about the stranger once more, which was stupid and pointless; she would probably never see him again. She went to sleep feeling a little sad because of it.

with the speed of long practice, and reflected, as she
brushed her hair, that it had been a period of luck that
she had been wearing the new suede shoes which
required her to walk carefully instead of hurry a week
ago, and although it was only April, it was pouring

CHAPTER TWO

SHE SAW HIM the following morning. It was Sister's
day off, so Augusta was to go on duty at eleven and
stay on until the night staff came on—a long day, but
normal enough. She had rushed out to shop soon after
breakfast and they had arrived together at the entrance
to the hospital, she on her feet, he at the wheel of a
dark grey Silver Shadow convertible. The big car
purred past her and stopped without sound, and after
one startled look she nodded coolly and flew up the
steps and past the porter's lodge, making for the back
of the entrance hall. She wasn't quite quick enough.
She was only half way across the gleaming linoleum
floor when he caught up with her.

He said silkily, 'Are you running away, or—er—
discouraging me?'

They had come to the passage running at right an-
gles to the hall. Augusta took the right-hand fork, and
found him still beside her.

'Neither,' she snapped a little breathlessly. 'I've
been out shopping and I'm due on duty in ten
minutes.'

She heard him chuckle. 'And first you must get
your breath back,' he remarked with mock sympathy.
They had reached the end of the passage and he
opened the door which gave on to the inner courtyard,
across which loomed the austere lines of the Nurses'
Home. Augusta fled through it with a muttered
'Goodbye', not looking at him at all. She changed

with the speed of long practice, and reflected, as she brushed her hair, that it had been a piece of luck that she had been wearing the new jersey dress which matched her eyes. She had bought it barely a week ago, and although being early April, it was possibly a little cool to have worn it, the sun had been shining. Then she had got out the black patent leather handbag her father had given her for her last birthday. It was to find shoes to match this treasured article which had her out so early. She had found its exact match at Raynes, and had had the elegant slingbacks on her feet when they met. The fact somehow compensated for the fact that he drove a Rolls-Royce.

She took the report from another part-time staff nurse, a girl she had known well before she had left to get married a year previously. They had a cup of coffee together once the Kardex was dealt with, and Augusta questioned cautiously, 'Are there any visitors on the floor?'

'Mother's in One.' This with an expressive lifting of eyebrows. 'There's a beautiful creature with Lady Belway—in a white dress, ducky, with one of those tapestry belts that cost the earth. T-strap lizard shoes and handbag to match...' The two young women stared at each other, wanting the unobtainable for a few unguarded moments, then, 'There's someone with the Brig—a downtrodden-looking female of uncertain age.'

They giggled together, but not unkindly. 'No one else?' asked Augusta.

'No one else. And a good thing too, you'll be able to get the rest of the bits and pieces done before lunch, and then catch up on the paper work during the afternoon.' Babs got to her feet. 'Well, I'm off

home to clear up and get a meal for James. Thank
heaven it's pay-day, I've gone through the housekeeping again.' She turned to go. 'How's Archie?'
she asked over her shoulder. Augusta was aware, a
little uncomfortably, that the hospital took Archie and
her for granted. She said:

'We went to the Regent last night, to see that new
film…he's fine.'

She was looked at intently from the door. 'Love's
young dream wearing a bit thin?'

Augusta gave the bib of her apron a twitch. She
said mildly, 'Well, you know, Babs, it never was
love's young dream—we just get on well together.'
She smiled a little ruefully. 'Look, if you were a
struggling houseman with no money and his way to
make, would you fall in love with me?'

'No, I wouldn't—but there again, I can quite see
that someone might. You're no beauty, Gussie, but
you look different. 'Bye.'

Left to herself, Augusta wasted a few minutes looking at her reflection in the tiny mirror which was all
Sister Cutts allowed herself. Babs was right, she was
no beauty. She sighed, and went to see what everyone
was doing. The work was going smoothly, at least for
the nurses, but the ward maid had a great deal to say
about the orderly pinching her newest duster when
she hadn't been looking—a trivial matter which took
a few minutes to unravel and smooth over by the
simple expedient of getting another duster from the
cupboard and awarding it to the maid. Augusta was
aware that upon Sister's return she would have to account for its absence from the neat pile so jealously
guarded under lock and key. She had learned long
ago that Ward Sisters tended to regard their stock of

floor polish, Vim, scrubbing brushes, soap and the
like as if they were priceless treasures to be kept in
safe custody for ever and ever. She thought it possible
that they suffered real pain when asked to part with
a single one of these items. She shrugged aside the
small matter of the duster; doubtless before Sister got
back, she would have to raid the cupboard again.
Then she began her round of the patients, but she had
barely opened Marlene's door when Matron arrived.
She was a small woman, and pretty, with curly hair
and blue eyes, and could have been any age between
forty and fifty. She looked attractive in uniform and
the frilly cap she affected—and at the hospital dances
she was positively glamorous. She smiled now and
said, 'Ah, Staff Nurse,' and Augusta, replying suitably, marvelled that anyone so soft and feminine could
be so intimidating, and, when it was required of her,
inflexible too—as she had been over the question of
Augusta staffing on PP.

'Just a quick round, Staff Nurse Brown—I'm sure
you're busy.' And Augusta once more opened the
door of Number One, hoping the while that the student nurses hadn't popped into the sluice for a natter.
Matron was wonderful; she cut through the grumbling
and complaining about the wrong kind of tea and eggs
that were too hard-boiled, and all the other small
grievances uttered, with the precise skill of a sharp
pair of scissors cutting silk; but to the slightest whim
of the really ill she lent an attentive ear, listening with
kindness and sympathy and suggesting remedies, conveying to the patient as she did so her complete con-
fidence in Staff Nurse Brown to bring about any
change for the good of those she was looking after.
The Brigadier was very difficult. Augusta supposed

that the depressing-looking female with him was his daughter—it seemed strange that such a vigorous, short-tempered man could be the father of someone so spiritless, but perhaps he had made her so. As they entered he was talking to her in a subdued roar, which changed to a jovial boom when he saw them.

'Good morning, dear lady.' This to Matron, and then as his eye fell upon Augusta, 'And you too, young woman.' He fixed Matron with a still alert and gallant eye. 'Of all the nurses here, she's the only one who knows how to carry on a conversation—understands cricket, too, and makes a good job of my damn foot.'

There was a tiny pause, for everyone in the room knew that on the following morning the Brigadier and his damn foot were to part company for ever in the operating theatre.

Augusta spoke quickly, almost stammering in her sympathy. The Brig was bad-tempered and irascible, but he had the courage of a lion in his eighty-year-old body. She asked inanely, 'What do you think of the change in the Test team, Brigadier?' and saw Matron's glance; perhaps she was making a fool of herself, but could imagine how the old man felt under the façade of ill-humour. He clutched the lifeline of conversation she had offered, and they embarked on five minutes of cricket. Outside the door once more, Matron remarked, 'Nursing is hard sometimes, is it not, Nurse Brown?' and smiled rather nicely. Augusta knew what she meant; it wasn't long hours and tired feet or hurried meals to which she referred, but the hardness of not being able to help.

Lady Belway still had a visitor. Augusta, under cover of Matron's polite conversation, verified that

the shoes really were lizard; she also looked to see if
there was an engagement ring, to be thwarted by the
fact that there was a ring on every finger.

Of the owner of the Rolls-Royce there was no sign.
He must have been earlier and gone again. Augusta
experienced a sense of disappointment out of all pro-
portion to the occasion while she listened with half
an ear to Lady Belway crossing swords with Matron
over the vexed question of the lack of pepper in the
cucumber sandwiches she had been offered for the
previous day's tea.

The day passed quickly, divided as it was into seg-
ments, each of which was stuffed to capacity with a
variety of jobs to be done—and done properly whatever the setbacks and interruptions; and there were
many. The girl, after spending most of the morning
with Lady Belway, went away just before lunch, and
Augusta, helping the old lady back to bed, hoped that
she might talk about her visitors, but she was too
occupied in complaining about the books which had
arrived from Mudies.

Augusta took the Brigadier to Theatre the next
morning, because she had promised him that she
would. He was more peppery than ever, but she didn't
allow this to make any difference to the steady flow
of conversation on her part. Usually patients going to
Theatre, unless too ill to care, wanted to talk about
trivialities—not so the Brig, who behaved much as
though he was preparing for battle—as indeed he was.
Even his pre-med did little to dull his sharp old wits,
and he was still telling her about the drop in his steel
shares as they started off in careful procession down
the corridor. Only as they waited for the lift did he

catch hold of her hand and ask tersely, 'I wonder where I shall wake up?'

To which Augusta replied in a deliberately matter-of-fact manner:

'In your bed, with my gimlet eye upon you.'

He gave a cackle of laughter. 'Not gimlet—gorgeous!'

They laughed together, and sailed down in the lift, his hand still fast held in her small, comforting one.

Theatre block was on the floor below. They had almost reached its heavy swing doors, when they opened and the man who so occupied her unwilling thoughts came through them. She was surprised to see him there until she remembered that he had probably been to see Mr Weller-Pratt, though it was a strange place to see a consultant surgeon. Still, it was none of her business...but she did feel it was her business when he stopped by the trolley and said cheerfully, 'Hullo, Brigadier—into the jaws of death, eh?'

She thought the remark in the worst possible taste, but apparently the Brig found it funny, for he chuckled and said hazily:

'Hullo, my boy—it won't be for the first time, either.'

Augusta said austerely, 'The patient is under sedation—kindly leave him quiet.'

But the big man, looming beside her so disturbingly close, made no apology. Instead he said softly, 'Ah, the guardian angel, of course.' He grinned at the Brigadier, smiled with great charm into her outraged face, winked, and went on down the corridor, his steps very light for such a large man. And they went through the swing doors then, into the little world of

sterile quiet, faintly redolent of anaesthetics; which
was the operating theatre.

'Decent young fellow,' murmured the Brig as she
took away his pillow and started to roll up the sleeve
of his theatre gown, ready for the anaesthetist's needle. She asked, casually, her heart beating a little faster, because she was going to know who the man was
at last.

'Who is he, Brigadier?'

He focused his old eyes upon her and began, in a
woolly voice, 'Godson of an old friend...' He closed
his eyes, and she heaved a resigned sigh as she turned
away to get his chart for the theatre nurse. She wasn't
going to find out after all.

She was by the Brigadier's bedside when he
opened his eyes again, and before he had time to become confused, said at once:

'Hullo there. You're back in bed—everything's
fine; you can go to sleep.' She smiled and nodded at
him and gave him her hand and was satisfied at the
strength of the squeeze he gave it. He had stood the
operation very well. Presently she was relieved by
another nurse and went along to the dining room for
her dinner, but she was late and it had been kept hot
for her and tasted of nothing at all. She went back to
the ward and made tea, and then, revived, set about
the afternoon's work. The day seemed very long, perhaps because the sun was shining so brightly out of
doors and she was imprisoned. She felt a little mean,
thinking it; probably the patients felt just as she did,
and with far more reason. But they could at least give
vent to their discontent—and did. The worst of them
was Lady Belway, who refused to be satisfied by anything at all, from the colour of her pills to the ar-

rangement of the vast number of flowers in her room,
and it was no use telling her that the staff had too
much to do anyway... Augusta had just returned from
the old lady's room for at least the sixth time, and
was making a tardy start on the report, when there
was a knock on the door. Without looking round, she
said in a resigned voice, 'If that's the Brig's drip
stopped again...'

She looked over her shoulder and met pale blue
eyes. He stood just inside the door, as elegant and
self-possessed as always, smiling.

'What do you want?' she wanted to know ungra-
ciously, firmly ignoring the rush of excitement at the
sight of him.

He came a little further into the room. He was holding the largest bunch of tulips she had ever seen in
her life—on his way to visit Lady Belway, no doubt.
She glowered at him because she was tired and hungry and her hair needed doing.

He said blandly, 'You make me feel so welcome.
There's an old song; something about ''There is a
lady sweet and gentle''—or was it kind? I expect you
are too, only I seem to be on the wrong wavelength.'

He laid the tulips in all their profusion on the desk,
to blot out the Kardex and charts and laundry lists
and forms. 'These are for you—tulips for Miss Augusta Brown, because the sun has shone all day, and
I doubt if she has encountered even one sunbeam.'

He turned on his heel and at the door said over one
shoulder:

'By the way, do your thumbs prick each time we
meet? It seems to me that they should.'

He shut the door quietly, leaving her speechless.

The tulips caused a good deal of comment from the

night nurses when they came on duty. She explained, with a heightened colour, that one of the patients' visitors had left them for her, without mentioning who it was—and bore goodnaturedly with a little mild teasing before going off duty clasping their magnificence to her starched bosom.

She was halfway down the stairs when he caught up with her. She had known who it was, if not by the pricking of her thumbs, then by some sixth sense, but she didn't turn round, indeed, she contemplated breaking into a run, only to discard the idea as being undignified, so he caught up with her easily enough, observing mildly, 'What—too tired to run away?'

She smiled frostily and answered shortly, 'No,' and then remembered that he had, after all, been kind enough to give her the tulips.

'The flowers are lovely,' she said in a slightly less frigid voice. 'It was kind of you.'

They had reached the bottom of the stairs; she added 'I go this way.' She smiled a little and turned away, to be instantly caught and held by the large hand on her shoulder and twiddled round to face him again.

'Since we are saying goodnight—' he said softly, and bent to kiss her.

She spent a wakeful night, rehearsing the cool manner in which she would greet him when they next met. It was a pity that her lack of sleep was wasted, for he didn't come. After a week she was forced to admit to herself that the tulips had been in the nature of a farewell gesture, and that he was now probably building bridges or discovering oil wells in some far-flung spot of the globe. That he was no longer in London at least was obvious, because the dark-haired girl still came to visit Lady Belway, and Augusta had seen her leave the hospital, driving herself in a rakish little sports car. On the eighth day, she threw away the last of the tulips, designating, as it were, his memory to the dustbin of her mind. She had plenty of other things to fill it…the Brig, making good progress, was none the less very difficult, especially on the days when the cricketing news wasn't good. Miss Dawn Dewey, recovered rather reluctantly from her cold, had gone, to be replaced by a minor statesman with tonsilitis…and there had been a fresh batch of T's and A's in. Lady Belway, organised at last with a nurse to take her home and stay, was due to go. Augusta had been invited—rather, commanded, to visit her and take tea; something she was loath to do, but perhaps the old lady was lonely, and it would be interesting to see where she lived—somewhere off Knightsbridge, in one of the squares.

She had been surprised one day when the girl had stopped her as she left Lady Belway's room, and said, 'It's silly the way we see each other every day and don't know each other's names—at least, I know yours. I'm Susan Belsize—Lady Belway's niece.' She put out a hand, and Augusta shook it and said politely and a little absentmindedly, 'How do you do?' because she was thinking about Mrs Bewley the alcoholic, who had the first symptoms of pellagra; she was already having nicotine acid, but it obviously wasn't sufficient…she would have to telephone Dr Watts. She smiled vaguely at Miss Belsize, who, it seemed, wasn't in a hurry, for she went on, 'You've been very kind to my aunt. I expect you know that she wanted you to go home with her—but Matron said you were indispensable.' She added with a rather gushing sympathy, 'You must get so tired, and I'm sure you don't get much fun.'

Augusta thought she detected pity, and anyway what sort of fun did the girl mean? She said, a little extravagantly, that yes, she had quite a lot of fun, and edged towards the office door. But her companion, with time on her hands, seemed incapable of realising that there were those who worked. She observed archly:

'Of course, this place is stuffed with doctors, isn't it?' She shot a playful look at Augusta. 'We saw you out the other evening.'

Augusta blinked, trying to think of a mutual social background. Not a bus queue, surely, and certainly not the cheapest seats at the cinema, and the little café where Archie sometimes took her for coffee was hardly the kind of place Miss Belsize would be seen in. She said carefully, 'Oh? I don't think...'

'You were with one of the doctors—I'm sure I've seen him around. We passed you both as we were leaving one evening, rather late, but you didn't see us.'

'Us,' thought Augusta, 'the man with straw-coloured hair.' She murmured politely, her hand on the office door which she opened an inch or two, and her companion said with animation:

'You meet so many people, don't you? But I daresay you forget them...ships that pass in the night and all that stuff.' She laughed. She had a pleasant laugh.

'Oh, definitely,' said Augusta, her mind still on Mrs Bewley. 'I really must get on...you'll forgive me if I...?'

Miss Belsize said at once with a genuine concern, 'Oh, my poor dear, I'm keeping you from your work, aren't I absolutely beastly?' She giggled. 'I expect I shall see you again.'

She floated away down the corridor, leaving a faint delicious whiff of Chanel Number 5 on the air. Augusta gave an appreciative sniff before going to the telephone, and then forgot all about her, for the time being at least.

It seemed quiet on PP after Lady Belway had gone home. Augusta missed the old lady's caustic tongue and the autocratic voice demanding this, that and the other thing. She had been a trying patient, but an interesting person, and something Augusta didn't quite admit to herself, while she had been in the hospital, there had always been the chance that she would have visitors—which visitors, Augusta took care not to define. She supposed that she could have found out from the Brig the name of the man who had given her the tulips, but each time she was on the point of asking, something had prevented her from doing so. She decided that she wasn't meant to know anyway. He had been a ship that passed in the night, as Susan Belsize had so tritely put it. All the same, as she got off the bus outside Harrods a few days later, she hoped that Lady Belway might mention him.

Lady Belway lived in a Nash house; one of a terrace of houses making up one side of a quiet square within ten minutes' walk of Harrods. She rang its old-fashioned door bell and stood back to admire the window boxes decorating the downstairs rooms. The house was in a beautiful state of preservation, as was the elderly butler who presently opened the door, and led her, at his own pace, across the narrow hall and up a handsome staircase to the drawing room—an apartment which took up a major part of the first floor, with windows both back and front and a vast chimneypiece the focal point of its further wall. Lady Belway was lying on a day bed, swathed in a variety of pastel-coloured wraps and stoles, which showed up her white, elegantly dressed hair to perfection. The butler announced Augusta in a sonorous voice, making what he could of her prosaic name, and her hostess said with a good deal of pleasure, 'How nice to see you, Staff Nurse...no, I cannot possibly call you that—I shall call you Augusta. Come here and sit down beside me and tell me what you have been doing.'

Augusta, privately of the opinion that her activities would be both boring and distasteful to the old lady, took her seat on a Sheraton armchair near enough to her hostess to make conversation easy, and instead of answering her question, asked several of her own, which launched Lady Belway into a happy and somewhat rambling account of the delights of being in her own home once more.

Augusta had expected the nurse to be there, and perhaps Susan Belsize; but it soon transpired that the former was off duty for the afternoon, and the latter had flown over to Paris for a brief period.

'The dear gal needed a change after dancing attendance on me all the while I was in hospital,' explained Lady Belway. 'If it hadn't been for her and my godson, I should have been a lonely old woman.'

Augusta politely agreed, while she tried to remember a single day while Lady Belway had been in hospital when she had had no visitors at all. There were, she supposed, degrees of loneliness.

They spent an amicable afternoon together, taking tea in some state off Sèvres china and talking about a great many things; indeed, during a discussion on foreign politics, Lady Belway paused to comment that Augusta was a well-informed girl. She said this in some surprise, so that Augusta was moved to remind her that nurses were, on the whole, tolerably well educated and reasonably intelligent, which remark Lady Belway took in good part, saying graciously, 'And what is your father, Augusta?'

She forbore from making the obvious answer; instead: 'A veterinary surgeon,' she added, to save her interrogator from asking the next question. 'He has a large country practice.'

'Where?'

'On the Dorset-Somerset border.'

'And do you not prefer London?'

Augusta was emphatic. 'No, I don't, Lady Belway. But to make a success of nursing I had to train at a first-class hospital and now I have to get all the experience I can.'

'You wish to take a Sister's post?'

Augusta hesitated. 'Well, I suppose that's what I'll end up as.'

'Do you not wish to marry?'

She said evasively, 'Oh, yes,' and then because she was becoming annoyed by so many questions, she said, 'I'm afraid I must go...I'm on duty this evening.'

Lady Belway looked genuinely disappointed. 'I had hoped that you could have spent a few hours—however, if you must return.' She brightened. 'Supposing I were to telephone your Sister Cutts?'

Augusta, suppressing a smile at the thought of Sister Cutts' face if that were to happen, said seriously,

'I'm afraid that would be no good. You see, Sister expects to go off duty when I get back.'

'In that case,' said her hostess graciously, 'I must let you go. But I should like you to come again.'

Augusta said that yes, of course she would, and was completely taken aback when the old lady drew her down to kiss her cheek.

'You're a very nice gal,' she stated, and then a little wistfully, 'it's good of you to spare time for an old woman.'

This remark struck Augusta as rather pathetic; she said with perfect truth, 'But it's not like that at all. I enjoyed coming, and I should like to come again. I'm going home on holiday tomorrow, but I shall be back in a fortnight.'

Lady Belway smiled. 'I shall send you a note, and perhaps you will telephone me.'

They parted in mutual friendliness, and on the way downstairs, through the quiet house, Augusta reflected that quite possibly Lady Belway was lonely, despite her numerous acquaintances; probably her sharp tongue, and her distressing habit of saying exactly what she thought, precluded her from having many close friends.

The next day she got out of the train at Sherborne to find her mother waiting for her. They greeted each other with the warm casualness of deep affection, and went out to the car.

'Throw your luggage in the back, Roly,' her mother commanded, 'and I'd much rather you drove...your father had to go over to Bagger's Farm and Charles was just getting ready to fetch you when they sent a message for him to go to Windhayes—one of the Jersey herd, you know. So I went with him and brought the car on up here. He'll give us a ring at home when he's ready, and perhaps you'll fetch him.'

While she was talking, Mrs Brown had settled herself beside her daughter. Augusta was fidgeting around with the ignition key and the starter; she hadn't driven for almost three months; it was to get the feel of it again. The car was a Morris Traveller 1300, elderly and a little battered by reason of the fact that it was sometimes used for the transport of smaller animals. Augusta, as she got into gear, had a sudden vivid memory of the immaculate Rolls the man with the straw-coloured hair had been driving, and went faintly pink when her mother remarked observantly:

'What were you remembering, darling? It must have been something nice.' But she had taken care not to make it sound like a question, so that Augusta was able to say, 'Oh, nothing really—it's lovely to see you again. Tell me all the news.'

She eased the car neatly away from the vehicles around them, and drove through the little town, and presently, free of its compact and bustling heart, took the road through North Wooton and Bishops Caundle and then turned away to pass through Kingstag. She knew the way blindfold, but she didn't hurry, preferring to trundle along the quiet road while her mother obediently gave her all the news.

Her home lay on one side of a small valley between the hills around them, midway between two small villages, and well back from the road. The house was of stone, with narrow latticed windows with stone lintels and a front door which still retained its Tudor arch. A long, long time ago, local history had it that it had been a small manor house, unimportant compared with some of the mighty houses in that part of Dorset, but nevertheless a gem of a building. Augusta drove through the gate, which was never closed for convenience' sake, and stopped with nice precision before the door. 'I'll leave the car here,' she said, as they got out. 'It'll save time when Charles telephones.'

They went indoors, and presently, after she had unpacked in her own pretty bedroom, she went down to the kitchen, and carried the tea tray through to the sitting room on the other side of the flagstoned hall. There were flowers everywhere, and the furniture shone with well cherished age—it was a warm afternoon, but there was a small wood fire burning in the stone fireplace. She sighed contentedly. It was nice to be home again.

After tea, she wandered outside with Stanley, the spaniel, walking sedately at her heels and the two Jack Russell terriers, Polly and Skipper, running in circles before her. She crossed the garden and went through the wicket gate at its end into a small paddock, used for convalescing horses and ponies, and permanently inhabited by Bottom, the family donkey. He wandered towards her now, nosed out the carrot she had thoughtfully brought with her, and allowed her to pull his rough furry ears and throw an affectionate arm about his neck. After a while, she wandered back again and in through the kitchen door, to sit down at the kitchen table and peel apples and talk to her mother, with Maudie the persian cat on her knee, and Fred, the battered old outcast tomcat who had latched himself on to them years ago, sitting beside her. They gossiped quietly until she bestirred herself to answer the telephone and fetch Charles.

She spent the evening getting her things ready to go to Holland, but only after helping her father with his evening visits. Quite a few calls had come in during the afternoon. She drove him from one farm to the other and then back to the small surgery near the house, enjoying the unhurried routine. They sat a long time over supper that evening, for there was a lot to talk about. She hadn't been home for several months; there was a lot of local news to catch up on, and she had plenty to talk about too, and presently, when the talk turned to herself, her father asked, as he usually did when she went home:

'Well, Augusta, think of getting married yet?' Her mother said gently, 'How's Archie?'

Augusta bit into an apple with her excellent teeth. 'Fine—but don't get romantic about him, Mother. We like going out together, but he's got years and years of work ahead of him and he's ambitious, which means he'll probably marry a girl with lots of money. I think I'm destined to be an old maid!'

Which remark called forth a good deal of amused comment from her brother, a quiet. 'Yes, dear' from her mother and a grunt from her father.

The next day went very quickly—too quickly, she thought, as she put the final touches to her packing in the evening. It was surprising how delightfully occupied it was possible to be, with no clock to watch and no reports to write, and feverish planning of off duty. She had, indeed, strolled down to the village stores and made a few purchases for her mother—an undertaking enlivened by a long chat over the counter with the grocer and any customers who had chanced to come into the shop—and in the afternoon she had got out the car and driven her mother down to the

vicarage to join the committee organising the annual
jumble sale. She had helped the vicar's wife hand
round the tea, and passed the time of day with the
ladies present, most of whom had known her since
she was a baby. And occasionally, much against her
will, she had thought about the man who had sent her
tulips because the sun had been shining.

She thought about him again as she was going to
sleep that night; wondering where he was and what
he was doing. She wished she knew if he and Miss
Belsize were...she sought for the right expression,
and decided that 'emotionally involved' would do
very well. It was difficult to tell with those sort of
people. She didn't go too deeply into what sort of
people they were—the subject was unrewarding; she
pulled the blankets over her ears to shut out his too
well-remembered voice, and went to sleep.

Charles took her up to London the next day and
put her on the Harwich train and rather unexpectedly
kissed her goodbye. 'Have fun,' he said and they both
laughed, for staying with the great-aunts, pleasant
though it was, held few excitements. 'Good for your
Dutch,' he added, as the train gave a preliminary
shudder. 'I'll pick you up when you get back. 'Bye.'

She settled back in her seat and picked up *Vogue*,
which Charles had thoughtfully provided for her.

CHAPTER THREE

AUGUSTA, getting out of the train at Alkmaar, thought how nice it was to be in Holland again. She had forgotten how wide the sky could be, and how incredibly flat and peaceful the countryside was. And she was delighted too, that her Dutch, although a little rusty and slow, was still adequate. The station was a little way out of the centre of the small water-encircled town; she got herself a taxi, and spent the short ride rediscovering landmarks she had almost forgotten. Her great-aunts lived in a seventeenth-century house with a stepped gable in the heart of the bustling town; it was awkward by modern standards, with steep stairs, high ceilings and quantities of heavy furniture which needed constant polishing. But the bathroom and kitchen, though they might look old-world, were remarkably well equipped, and the house had the cosy air of having been built for comfort hundreds of years earlier, and having, through thick and thin, retained that comfort. Augusta loved it, and when, on occasion, she heard some sightseer or other remark upon its picturesque appearance, she was apt to swell with pride, even though her connections with it were extraneous.

Maartje opened the door—she had been cooking and cleaning and housekeeping for the aunts for as long as Augusta could remember, and excepting for her hair, which had faded from pale corn to silver,

41

she hadn't changed at all. They greeted each other like the old friends they were.

'Your aunts are in the little sitting room,' said Maartje, 'go straight in, Augusta, and I will bring the coffee.'

Augusta made her way down the passage, narrow and panelled and hung with china plates and dim portraits; and knocked on the door at its end, and obedient to the quiet voice which bade her enter, went in. Her aunts were sitting as they always sat. At the round table in the middle of the room, both very upright in their straight, overstuffed chairs. The table had a finely woven rug thrown across it, upon which rested a Delft blue bowl filled with fruit. The windows, small and narrow, were hung with thick dark red curtains, and the wooden floor, worn and polished with its age, was partly covered with hand-pulled rugs. It looked exactly the same as when she had last seen it, three years ago...so did her great-aunts. Probably their clothes were different, for they were sufficiently well provided for to indulge in varied wardrobes, but as they invariably had their new dresses made exactly as those they were wearing, it was difficult to know this. They wore a great deal of black, the material being always of the finest and they each wore a quantity of gold jewellery, inherited from their mother, who had inherited it from her mother, and so on back over several generations, so that their rings and brooches and delicate dangling earrings were quite valuable. Both ladies were tall—a good deal taller than their great-niece, and they wore their hair in identical buns, perched high on their heads.

Augusta greeted them warmly, for she was fond of them both—and they, she knew, were fond of her.

She stood patiently so that they might take a good look at her and comment on her looks and clothes, and she was pleased and not a little relieved when they approved of her new green coat and matching dress. Then, at their invitation, she took the coat off, and sat down between them as Maartje brought in the coffee and little biscuits called Alkmaarse Jongens. She sipped the delicious coffee and ate the Alkmaar boys, wondering, as she always did, why the Dutch had such picturesque names for their biscuits. She must remember to take some home with her...the thought put her in mind of all the messages she had been charged to deliver. She gave them now, stopping to search for a forgotten word from time to time, and occasionally muddling her verbs. When she had finished, Tante Marijna observed in a gentle voice that it was a good thing that she had come to pay them a visit, for, although her Dutch was fluent enough, her grammar was, at times, quite regrettable. Tante Emma, who was the younger of the two old ladies, echoed this in a voice even more gentle, adding the rider that her English accent was fortunately very slight.

'You shall do the shopping, Augusta, while you are with us—there is no better way of improving your knowledge of our language—and we will have a few friends in, so that you will have an opportunity to converse.'

Augusta smiled and said with genuine pleasure that that would be nice, and how about her going up to her room so that she could unpack the presents which she had brought with her. The old ladies looked pleased and a little excited, and she left them happily engaged in guessing what the presents would be, while she went upstairs to the room in which she always slept when she paid them a visit.

It was two flights up, and overlooked the street below—a rather small room, plainly whitewashed and furnished simply in the Empire style. The curtains were a faded blue brocade and the coverlet was of patchwork, made by the great-aunts' mother before she married. There were a variety of samplers upon the walls—Augusta knew them all by heart, as well as the histories of those who had stitched them. She walked slowly round the room, looking at each in turn—it was a little like meeting old friends again— then she unpacked quickly and took her armful of parcels downstairs; pale pastel woollen stoles for the old ladies, warm sheepskin slippers for Maartje, English chocolates and homemade marmalade and tins of chocolate biscuits, and some packets of their favourite tea from Jacksons in Piccadilly. By the time all these delights had been tried on and tasted and admired, it was lunch time. The old ladies had *Koffietafel* at noon each day—a meal of rolls and different sorts of bread, with cheese and sausage and cold meat and a salad arranged before each place upon a small silver dish—and of course, coffee. Augusta, who was hungry after her journey, ate with a healthy appetite which pleased the aunts, who were, as far as she could remember, the only members of her family who had not, at one time or another, made some reference to her delicate plumpness. She still remembered how, when she was a little girl, she had paid them a visit with her parents from time to time, and they had staunchly maintained that she was exactly as she should be, remarks which had endeared them for always to a small girl sensitive to the word fat, and possessed of a brother who teased.

The transient excitement of her arrival had died down by the evening, and when she got up the next morning, it was as though she had been integrated into the even tenor of their lives without any change in its placid routine. She went shopping after breakfast, and then, because there was no hurry, strolled down Houtil towards Laat, peering in shop windows until she fetched up in Vroom and Dreesman's store, wandering happily from one counter to the next, pricing tights and undies and even trying on a few hats. But it was still early, and although the aunts had coffee soon after ten o'clock each morning, she could always get a cup from Maartje later. She turned her steps towards the Weigh House, because it was Friday and May and the cheese market would be in full swing. It was still a little early in the year for tourists, but there was a small crowd watching the cheese porters in their white shirts and trousers and coloured straw hats, going briskly to and fro in pairs, each pair carrying a large curved tray piled with cheeses between them. She had seen it all a dozen times before, but she stood and watched now with as much pleasure as though it was for the first time. The carillon was playing from the Weigh House tower too—she listened to *Piet Hein* and other Dutch folk songs she had half forgotten and then lingered just a little longer so that she could watch, as the clock struck the hour, the little figures of knights on horseback, high up on the tower, come charging through their doors, lances raised, while the clarion trumpeted over them. It made her a little late getting back, but the excuse that she hadn't been able to leave the cheese market until the

clock had struck was quite sufficient for her aunts.
They were proud of their town and its traditions and
found it quite proper that she should have wanted to
renew acquaintance with one of her childhood's
pleasures.

The days resolved themselves into a slow, smooth
pattern of doing nothing much. Friends came to tea
or coffee, until one afternoon a car was hired and the
aunts, incredibly elegant, drove, with her between
them to Bergen, a large village on the edge of the
sand dunes bordering the North Sea, to visit family
friends. Augusta had been a little amused at their
sharp-eyed scrutiny of her person before they went.
She had put on another dress, the colour of caramel
and simply cut, with an important chain belt encir-
cling her slim waist, and offset by the jade earrings
her father had given her because they matched her
eyes. Apparently her appearance pleased them, for
they smiled in unison and nodded their old heads before embarking on the tricky business of getting into
the car.

The friends were elderly—a distant cousin and his
wife. Augusta sipped sherry and made polite talk in
her best Dutch and found herself wishing for a
slightly younger companion. Her wish was to be
granted, for presently the drawing room door was
thrown open and a young man came in. She guessed
he was a year or two older than herself, maybe
twenty-five or six, and barely had time to wonder who
he was before he had greeted everyone in the room
and was standing beside her with their hostess. He
was, it appeared, the son of another dear old friend.
'Pieter van Leewijk,' he murmured as they shook
hands, 'but call me Piet. I've heard about you, of

course, and I daresay we may have met years ago when we were children.'

He smiled charmingly, first at her, then at his hostess, accepted a glass of sherry, and steered Augusta over to the window. They stood side by side looking out across the broad road to the island of grass and trees in its centre, inhabited by a few small, graceful deer.

'Such a nice idea,' she remarked, 'deer living in the centre of the village.' She smiled at the young man, who wasn't looking at the deer but staring at her. He spoke in Dutch. 'You are fluent in our language—someone said you were a nurse. I always thought nurses were dowdy, worthy girls.'

She raised sable brows. 'Indeed? Perhaps you don't get around a great deal.'

He laughed. 'I was paying you a compliment.'

She decided that he was, but he sounded a little too sure of himself. She asked sweetly, 'And you—what do you do?'

'I'm a fashion photographer. You see, it was a compliment.' He smiled again and took her glass. 'More sherry?'

She shook her head. 'Tell me about your work—it sounds interesting.'

It wasn't. It took only a few minutes for her to realise that he wasn't interested in anything else but beautiful models and how much money he could make, and how quickly he could make it. They went in to lunch, and inevitably, she found herself sitting beside him, with the older members of the party beaming at her, delighted with themselves that they had produced such a nice young man to entertain her. Only he didn't; he wasn't interested in anything she had to say—it was sufficient for her to say Yes and No and look suitably impressed. All the same, she tried her best to like him, for he was probably the only young man she would meet while she was in Alkmaar. He might even ask her out, and being a fair-minded girl, she was quite prepared to admit that she wasn't quite as groovy as the models. Probably he found her dull—all the same, if he did ask her out, she thought she would go.

He said carelessly, 'You shouldn't wear these new long skirts—they're for tall, slim girls—long legs and...' His eyes swept over her. They were eating a rich ice pudding with a great deal of cream. Augusta checked a desire to throw her portion into his smiling face.

She said crisply in English, 'Of all the insufferable, conceited bores that I've met, you're easily the prize specimen! How dare you tell me what to wear, and—and criticize my legs? Keep your shallow-brained remarks for the bird-witted creatures you purport to photograph.'

She smiled at him, her eyes like green ice, and was pleased to see him getting slowly red. She had been rude, but then so had he...and she had enjoyed every word of what she had said.

'Perhaps you don't know that I have a very good knowledge of English?' he queried stiffly.

'Why, I counted on that,' she said quietly. She flipped her eyelashes at him, smiled without warmth and said for the benefit of anyone who might have paused to listen to them, 'How delicious this pudding is—how lucky I am not to have to diet.'

They went back to the drawing room soon afterwards and she allowed herself to be drawn into a conversation on the subject of cheeses with her host, and later, when she took her departure with her two great-aunts and everyone was shaking everyone else by the hand, she allowed hers to rest a bare second in Pieter van Leewijk's, and under cover of the hum of fare-wells, murmured, 'Goodbye, Piet. So interesting meeting you,' and gave him a naughty smile before turning away.

On the way back to Alkmaar, the old ladies, on either side of her, discussed their outing. 'Such a pleasant young man,' remarked Tante Emma guile-lessly, 'perhaps he invited you out, *liefje*?'

'No, Tante Emma, Pieter is a busy young man, you know…he's going back to Utrecht this evening.' She saw their old faces drop—they had always wanted her to marry a Dutchman. 'I daresay he'll be back,' she added gently. 'He told me a great deal about his work,' and was rewarded by their pleased faces.

They were almost home when Tante Marijna com-plained of feeling a little sick. Augusta thought that the excitement of the day and the rather rich food they had eaten might be the cause; all the same, she asked a few pertinent questions—the aunts were nearly eighty and were of the generation which stoically con-cealed goodness knows what behind a well-bred ret-icence—but the old lady would admit to no pain or headache or tingling of the fingers. Nonetheless, she readily agreed to go to bed early, and when Augusta suggested that weak tea and a *bischuit* would suit a queasy stomach, agreed to that too, and when Augusta went to see her, last thing before she went to her own bed, she looked comfortable enough, and assured her niece that she would sleep all night.

It was in the small hours of the morning that Augusta was wakened by Tante Emma, wrapped untidily in a voluminous dressing gown and looking quite distraught. 'Your dear aunt,' she said, a little wildly. 'She's ill—dying, I believe.'

Augusta got out of bed. She said in an instinctively soothing voice:

'All right, Tante Emma,' her mind already busy. That sickness—but there hadn't been any other symptoms unless Tante Marijna had been holding out on her. She flung her pale pink housecoat over its matching nightie, pushed her feet into heelless slippers, said a trifle breathlessly to her aunt, 'Don't hurry, darling—I'll go down,' and was off down the stairs, her bright hair flying, her feet making no sound on the thick carpet. Outside Tante Marijna's door she stopped and then went in with deliberate, calm steps and no trace of worry upon her face.

The old lady lay against her pillows, very pale. Her blue eyes were resolutely open while the sweat trickled slowly down her drawn face. Augusta went to the bedside, possessed herself of her aunt's hand and took her pulse, saying at the same time, 'Hullo, Tante Marijna—is there a pain in your chest?'

The lids dropped over the anxious blue eyes, giving her the answer she had expected. She said gently, 'Keep very still, darling—you're going to be all right, but I have to fetch the doctor.' She smiled reassuringly and turned to Tante Emma who had just come into the room.

'Will you stay here while I telephone him—is the number in the book on the hall table?'

Tante Emma nodded and Augusta flew down another flight of stairs and picked up the receiver. Dr van Lindemann—she noted the name and dialled the number.

The voice that answered her sounded alert and calm and merely stated its name and didn't interrupt at all while she gave her brief details, being careful to get the Dutch as correct as she could, although she fancied, thinking about it afterwards, that she might have muddled a few verbs. However, she must have made sense, for the voice said crisply that yes, he would be round in ten minutes.

She ran back upstairs and found Tante Marijna just the same and Tante Emma in quiet tears. She wiped the sweat from the former's face and the tears from Tante Emma's woebegone countenance, breathed a few words of reassurance once more, and took flight once again, this time to the top of the house, to Maartje's room. Maartje was a little deaf; it took a minute or two to make her understand, but once she did, she was at once her sensible quick-witted self. She listened carefully to what Augusta had to tell her and was already throwing back the bed-clothes as Augusta left the room. She had barely reached her aunt's room again when the front door bell pealed—just once and gently. The doctor. Once more she sped down the narrow staircase and flung open the door. He came into the hall, and the old-fashioned lamp, hanging from its high ceiling, shone on his straw-coloured hair, so that it appeared white. He stared at her from the pale blue eyes which had occupied her thoughts more often than she cared to think. He said, softly, 'Hullo, Miss Augusta Brown,' and she, speechless, led him upstairs, aware of a sudden delight despite her anxiety for her aunt.

It seemed he was no stranger to her aunts. Tante

Emma greeted him tearfully. 'Constantijn, I am so glad to see you—my sister...'

He smiled at her with great kindness. 'Why not go back to your room with Maartje—I'll come and see you presently.'

While he was talking he had been standing by the bed, looking at his patient, who stared back at him and presently smiled very faintly at him. He smiled back warmly, and gently pressed the hand he was holding. He said quietly and with great calmness, 'I'm going to have a look at you—I believe I know what is wrong, but I must be sure, then you shall have something to take away the pain and allow you to sleep. When you wake up you will feel better.'

He set about his examination and Augusta helped him, because it was the natural thing to do, even without her cap and apron, and he seemed to expect it anyway. When he had finished, he opened his bag and took out a phial of morphia and presently slid a needle gently into Tante Marijna's arm. The old lady's eyes slid from his impassive face to Augusta's and back again.

'I absolutely refuse to go to hospital,' she said in a clear thready voice.

'I hadn't thought of it,' said Dr van Lindemann. 'Why should you when you've a perfectly good nurse here?'

His glance flickered across the bed. 'Stay here a moment, will you, while I talk to your aunt?' He didn't wait for her nod, but disappeared through the door, to reappear presently with Maartje.

'Maartje will sit here for a short while...there are a few things... I've given Juffrouw van den Pol some trichloral; I think she'll settle.' He glanced at the bed.

'Your aunt will be all right, I think. Maartje tells me there's coffee in the kitchen—come down and have a cup while we decide what to do.'

Augusta followed him meekly, and found the coffee pot warm on top of the stove; there was milk in a double saucepan too, hot enough to have a creamy coat wrinkling its surface. The doctor strolled around the kitchen collecting cups and saucers and a sugar pot, talking as he did so.

'Your aunt's had an attack of angina—just as you thought—nasty enough, but she'll recover. She's as fit as a woman of half her age and has great determination. Five days' complete bed rest and then gradual convalescence.'

Augusta nodded, the coffee pot in one hand, the milk in the other.

'Do you like the skin?' she inquired.

He looked as though he was going to laugh. 'Yes—do you?'

She began to pour. 'Yes. You'd better have it as you're the guest.'

'How nicely you put it,' he said smoothly. 'We'll share.'

They sat down opposite each other on the rush-seated wooden chairs that any museum would have been glad to possess. 'How long are you staying?' He was the doctor again, deliberate and detached.

She told him.

'That should be long enough to get her up and about again, provided all goes as it should. It will give me time to get hold of a nurse before you go. When did you get here?'

She told him that too, and added seriously, 'My

aunt hasn't done too much—I mean, they're always glad to see me, but I don't excite them.'

'As to whether you excite anyone or not is a matter of opinion.'

She saw the corner of his mouth twitch and knew that he was laughing at her, and went pink, but when he spoke again, his tone was impersonal.

'Could you manage to stay up for the rest of the night? There's not much of it left.'

She nodded, 'Yes, of course,' and he continued, 'Now, tell me, did your aunt do anything out of the way today—excitement—food—worry?'

She went over the day's happenings with the same care that she would have given to a ward report, but there wasn't much to learn from them, only the nausea in the car on the way home. She got up and put the cups in the sink and the milk and coffee back on the stove and they went back upstairs again, and while he checked his now sleeping patient's pulse and BP he sent Maartje down for coffee and gave Augusta some last-minute instructions, standing by the bed, looking at the old face on the pillows, peaceful once more and quite a good colour. Presently he nodded, well satisfied, and went across the landing to Tante Emma's room, to come back almost at once to say that she was asleep.

'Get Maartje to bed,' he suggested, 'then you will be able to get an hour or so yourself in the morning.'

Augusta agreed politely, privately of the opinion that she wouldn't be able to do anything of the sort—someone would have to stay with the patient, someone would have to shop and get the meals and keep Tante Emma company. Doubtless the problem would sort itself out in the morning.

Maartje had come upstairs again. The doctor took a last look at Tante Marijna and said, 'I'll leave you some trinitrate—you know what to do if she has another attack—but I want to know at once.'

He closed his bag and got up to go and Augusta followed him downstairs once more—the Friesian clock on the wall at the bottom of the staircase struck five as they passed it; the night was almost over. He opened the door and she said suddenly, because the thought had only just struck her:

'You weren't surprised to see me.'

He paused with his hand on the door; if he was irritable at this further, trivial delay to keep him from his bed, he showed no sign. He said, speaking English for the first time that night:

'I knew your voice.'

'But I was speaking Dutch.'

She saw the twitch come and go. 'My dear girl, I should know your voice anywhere, in whatever language you chose to speak—which reminds me, I must give you some lessons on Dutch verbs. You had them in a hopeless tangle!'

He was gone, leaving her in the dim early morning light. She would have liked to think about what he had just said; but there was no time just then.

He was back in three hours' time, during which period she had contrived to get the household organised. Maartje had crept down soon after seven and had taken Augusta's place by her aunt's bed, while she bathed and dressed with a speed which didn't permit of make-up or a hair-do. She tied her tresses back with a ribbon and ran back to her aunt, peeping in at Tante Emma on the way. She was still asleep—Augusta hoped that she would go on sleeping for sev-

eral hours. She had remembered that a daily woman
came in three days a week to help with the house-
work—if she could be persuaded to come every day,
that would give Maartje time to do the shopping and
cooking, and herself free to look after Tante Marijna,
as well as bear Tante Emma company. She suggested
this tentatively to Maartje, who approved; Mevrouw
Blom would be coming shortly, she would arrange
something with her. She hurried away to dress, and
presently put her silvery head round the door with the
whispered promise of breakfast.

Tante Marijna was showing signs of rousing. Augusta had taken her pulse and found it to be improved—her colour was better too, and her skin felt
dry and faintly warm. She started tidying the room,
pausing at the mirror to look at herself. She was a
little pale, and without powder and lipstick her face
looked very young—she gave her hair a vexed tweak;
it looked hideous, dragged back from her face all any-
how; she would find time to do it properly before Dr
van Lindemann arrived. Having decided which, it
hardly added to her good humour when he came,
light-footed and very fast, up the stairs only a minute
or so later.

He said '*Dag*, my dear Miss Brown,' and raked her
from head to foot with his sharp, pale gaze, but he
said nothing else, only turned at once to the bed, asking over one shoulder, 'She's not been conscious?'
He possessed himself of Tante Marijna's wrist. 'She
looks as though she's coming round.'

'She stirred a little about half an hour ago,' said
Augusta, 'but I've not tried to rouse her.'

'Good girl. Fluids for today, and as little movement
as possible—I'll leave you to see to washing and

feeding and so forth. You'll need several things, though, if she's to be nursed here. I'll give you a note for van Dijk, the *apotheek* on the corner—you know him? He'll let you have all you need.'

He turned back to the bed to find Tante Marijna's blue eyes looking at him, and spent the next five minutes explaining in a calm, exact manner what had been the matter with her and what he proposed to do to put it right. When he had finished, she whispered with a smile:

'What a nuisance I am, Constantijn—my apologies; and poor Augusta—it's her holiday.' She frowned. 'Perhaps I should go into hospital.'

Augusta shook her head. 'Of course not—you'll be on your feet long before I go home,' which was a little exaggerated, but who cared about that, so long as her aunt was put at ease? 'Besides,' she observed, 'I shall like looking after you.'

Her great-aunt smiled again. 'Dear child, but what about that nice Pieter—if he should want to take you out?'

Augusta found herself blushing, which was all the more annoying because the doctor was staring at her. 'I told you, Tante Marijna, he's gone back to Utrecht.'

'Oh, well, in that case…it will be delightful if you will look after me, Augusta.'

She closed her eyes and the doctor prepared to go, saying merely:

'I leave you in capable hands, Juffrouw van den Pol.' And then, 'See me to the door, if you will, Miss Brown.'

She obeyed this somewhat highhanded request, but only, she told herself, because he might wish to tell her something about her aunt.

He didn't. Halfway down the stairs he asked, 'Who's Pieter?'

She came to a halt, and he half turned, lounging against the carved wood banisters. 'Whatever business is it of yours?' she wanted to know.

He raised a pale eyebrow. 'But of course it's my business I shouldn't like you to pine away through lack of seeing your boy-friends.'

'He's not my boy-friend,' she snapped. She hadn't meant to tell him, but she was annoyed, so that common sense played no part in her answer.

'He's a ghastly young man I met yesterday at Bergen—a photographer of models and clothes and suchlike stuff, and full of himself.' She paused to draw a furious breath. 'He dared—he actually dared—to…to criticise my dress because I'm not the right shape…' She stopped, choking back rage, eyeing the man on the stair below her. If he dared to laugh! He did no such thing, but said mildly, 'I should have thought your shape would be—er—exactly right for any vagary of fashion.' He added with interest, 'I imagine you dealt with him?'

Her green eyes lighted up with satisfaction. 'Yes, I told him that he was an insufferable conceited boor, and other things besides.'

He gave her a considered look. 'I don't think that I number this Pieter among my acquaintances, but I can find it in my heart to be sorry for him. I don't suppose he stood a chance.' He turned on his heel and started on down the stairs. 'I'll be in some time this evening. *Dag.*'

The house seemed empty when he had gone, possibly because he was such a large man that the small rooms tended to be crowded when he was in them.

Augusta sighed without knowing it, and went to the kitchen to make the weak tea he had prescribed for his patient.

The day went smoothly. Tante Marijna continued to improve, and Tante Emma, once she was awake and had been convinced that her sister was alive and likely to stay so, became quite cheerful, and even derived some satisfaction from doing little things to help around the house. All the same, despite Mevrouw Blom's willingness to help out, Augusta found it quite impossible to get even an hour's sleep. By evening time she was so sleepy that the voices around her had taken on a dreamlike quality, either very loud or very soft, and none of them making much sense. It was bliss when Tante Marijna dropped off into a light doze and Maartje and Tante Emma had gone down to the kitchen to prepare the evening meal. Augusta allowed her heavy lids to droop, only to drag them agonisingly open as the front door bell pealed. Another peal like that one and Tante Marijna would start awake. She glanced at the old lady, still quietly sleeping, and listened for footsteps below, but presumably the ladies in the kitchen hadn't heard, and if it had been the doctor, he would have opened the door and brought himself upstairs. She went down to the door, yawning. The boy outside, waiting, grinned cheerfully and thrust an enormous bouquet at her. Tulips—golden tulips; dozens of them. She took them from him, hunted on the hall table for some small change, pressed it into his hand, shut the door quietly and went upstairs again, clasping the tulips. Her aunt was still sleeping; she made sure of that before she turned her attention to the small white envelope tucked in with the flowers. It was addressed to herself in the same untidy scrawl in which the note to the *apotheek* had been written.

Her first feeling had been one of relief, because on the way upstairs she had been beset with the dreadful idea that they might have been from Pieter van Leewijk; now she opened the envelope with mixed feelings which she didn't pause to analyse, drew out the card and read:

'I shall call for you tomorrow afternoon at two o'clock if you are agreeable to a short run in the car.'

It was signed C. van Lindemann. She read it again, just to make sure that that was what he had written. It was, and she found herself a little disconcerted at this somewhat businesslike invitation. All the same, she knew that she would accept—he would presumably mention it when he next came; it would give her a chance to find out something about him, and there would be time enough afterwards to tell him that she had found his note a trifle peremptory. There was quite a lot she wanted to know. She supposed that he lived in Alkmaar, for he obviously had a practice—but he seemed equally at home in London, and he had told her that Lady Belway was his godmother—and where did Susan Belsize fit in? She sat engrossed in speculation, some of it somewhat wild, until her aunt's voice startled her.

'Those beautiful flowers! They're yours, Augusta?'

She admitted that they were, and when her aunt wanted to know who had sent them, said with extreme nonchalance, 'Well, actually, they're from Doctor van Lindemann.'

Tante Marijna murmured, 'Just so, child. Put them in water—I am quite well enough to be left for a few minutes.'

Which Augusta did, filling the old house with their fragrance and colour.

She thanked the doctor later that evening, after he had seen Tante Marijna and pronounced her better, with the corollary that she was still to do absolutely nothing for the next few days. Augusta accompanied him to the door, where she said a little coolly because he had made no mention of their outing, 'Thank you for the tulips—the whole house is full of them.'

He gave her a bright glance, and on the point of speaking, said nothing, but opened the door and then bent and kissed her lightly on her mouth, and had gone, shutting the door quietly behind him, before she could so much as draw breath.

She wasn't tired any more. She went back to her aunt's room and gave her the small amount of supper she was allowed, and then prepared her for the night, and presently, with Maartje to take her place, went to her own room. It was after she had returned and was sitting by her aunt's bed that she noticed the old lady's distress. She caught up an old frail hand and gave it a reassuring squeeze and asked:

'What is it, Tante Marijna? Something's worrying you.'

Her aunt hesitated. 'It is very foolish of me, but I find that I am a little afraid of being here alone—just during the night, you know.'

'You're not,' said Augusta instantly, and dismissing the blissful thought of sleep. She had had some hazy notion of spending the night in the little room across the landing, once Tante Marijna had settled for the night, but this was obviously out of the question. 'It's all arranged,' she went on mendaciously, 'I'm going to bath and undress, and come back here and make myself comfy for the night in this chair. I've heaps of letters to write and I'm not a bit sleepy. I'll fetch Maartje.'

That sensible woman, when appealed to, agreed that there was nothing else to do. 'Perhaps if Juffrouw van den Pol sleeps you will be able to close your eyes,' she observed hopefully. 'I am glad the doctor has arranged to take you out tomorrow—you can do with a little outing.'

Augusta, swallowing coffee, choked. 'Oh, but he has said nothing to me.'

'Nevertheless, it is all arranged. Mevrouw Blom will stay until five o'clock and I shall sit with the patient. The doctor has given me the telephone number of a doctor should anything happen, so you have no need to worry.' She beamed at Augusta. 'It is wonderful to have you here, for we are now three old women and not very good at looking after ourselves when we are not well. Now I will go upstairs and sit with your aunt while you prepare yourself for the night.'

The night was very long—Augusta, filled with the false energy of overtiredness, wrote several letters, pausing for gentle chat from time to time until her aunt was lulled into a sense of security and closed her eyes, leaving her free to read. She had prudently combed the house for reading matter earlier in the evening; now she picked up *De Telegraaf* and read it conscientiously from cover to cover, thinking smugly how much it would improve her Dutch. This salve to her conscience having been achieved, she opened up a paperback she had begged from Maartje, only to find that she had already read it in English under another title. She flung it down rather crossly, and crept

across the room to look at the few books on her aunt's
bedside table: the Bible, Jacob Cats, Pieter de Vries
and Joost van den Vondel. She chose Cats and Vondel
and spent the next few hours alternating between the
former's easily understood poetry about ordinary,
everyday things and people; and the latter's lofty
tragic sagas about Biblical characters.

But by one o'clock she had had enough of seventeenth-century poetry, and her aunt was sleeping
soundly. She went quietly from the room and stole
through the quiet house to the kitchen, where she
gathered together a trayful of odds and ends to eat,
and bore them, with a mug of coffee, upstairs. The
meal revived her; she picked up Cats again, but after
a little while her attention began to wander, so that
she closed the book and gave herself up to her
thoughts, which were largely of Doctor van Lindemann and becoming more and more hazy. She had
told herself sternly that evening that she would ignore
his kiss—she had been kissed before, and there was
nothing unusual in it. She repeated this several times,
uneasily aware that even if he hadn't found it unusual,
it had affected her in some strange way. She tried to
decide exactly how this could be, and fell asleep in a
woolly cloud of half dreams, which, like all dreams,
made complete sense.

She awoke an hour later—it was almost five
o'clock and the dawn was already paling the lamp-
light in the bedroom. She got up, yawning and
stretching and feeling more tired than ever. Perhaps,
now that Tante Marijna had had a good night's sleep,
she wouldn't mind her sleeping close by, within call.
She crept around the house, making tea and eating an
apple while she waited for the kettle to boil, and pres-

ently, much refreshed, she washed and dressed with a good deal of coming and going to make sure that her patient was still sleeping.

The first pale sunshine was creeping over the street outside as she once more took her seat by her aunt's bed. That lady wakened half an hour later, feeling much better, and as a consequence, inclined to be peevish because she wasn't allowed to get up, let alone wash herself. However, the promise of a light breakfast and something a little more interesting for lunch put her in a better humour, and the morning proceeded comfortably enough. Augusta, breakfasted and fresh from a visit to the kitchen to confer with Tante Emma on the day's meals, reached the front door in time to open it for Doctor van Lindemann. He said '*Dag*,' and subjected her to a cool stare which she was beginning to find disconcerting.

'No sparkle this morning?' he inquired lightly. He stood beside her, wearing the slightly smug air of a well-rested, well-fed man who was pleased with himself and his world. Augusta thought sourly of her wakeful night. Hashing verbs and tenses into icy Dutch, she said coldly, 'You appear to be confusing me with one or other of your numerous acquaintances,' which remark for some reason made him shake with laughter. 'Never,' he said at last, 'never shall I confuse you with any—er—other female.' He allowed his gaze to rest upon the pale copper of her hair, so that she pinkened with anger, but before she could speak: 'How's our patient?' he asked in a suddenly professional, lofty tone which gave her no opportunity to vent her ill-humour.

She became a nurse again, standing beside the bedside while he examined his patient at some length, quelled the old lady's impatient wish to get up and make sure that the house was being run properly, and advised her to do as she was told for the time being, because it was the only way in which to get better quickly. 'I'm going to take your niece out this afternoon,' he continued, 'a run in the fresh air will do her good. I have arranged for you to be looked after for an hour or two. I'll pick her up at two o'clock.'

He smiled charmingly at her and then at Augusta, who hadn't been expecting it and scowled across the bed at him because he was arranging everything without having bothered to find out if she wanted to go. He ignored the scowl and said cheerfully, 'Ready at two, then,' and took himself off.

She had had to hurry to be ready for him. The aunts, bless them, had very little sense of time. She would have liked to have done something elaborate with her hair, and spend more than a few scrambled minutes on her face. She flung on the dress she had worn to Bergen, aware that the front door bell had sounded at least five minutes earlier. He would have to wait! When she arrived in the sitting room, she had half expected some comment upon her tardiness, but he said nothing at all, beyond wishing Tante Emma a polite goodbye. The Rolls-Royce was outside, taking up a great deal of space in the narrow street. He ushered her into its comfort and got in beside her, and because she was very aware of him, she said hastily, 'What a lovely car, but is it practical for Alkmaar—all these narrow streets?'

'I don't use it for the practice—I've a Mini, but this one's useful for long trips.' She gave him a rather startled look. 'And for taking out pretty girls,' he added suavely.

She said, a little breathless, 'Thank you for boosting my morale, but I'm not pretty, you know.'

He trickled the big car down to the end of the street and turned into the town's main thoroughfare, past the great St Lawrence church and out on to the road to Bergen. Only then did he say, 'Allow me to be the best judge of that.' He then began to talk about nothing in particular. She had liked his voice; now she thought that she had never heard one so quiet and soothing as his. She said very little, because there was no need and she was sleepy. Her eyelids became too heavy to hold open any longer—she would have to close them just for a moment. She did so, and slept.

When she opened them again, she was lying comfortably within the circle of his arm, her head resting on his shoulder. She sat up, putting an instinctive hand up to her hair. It felt all right. She looked at him sideways, and said contritely, 'Oh, dear, I am sorry. I didn't mean to go to sleep, truly I didn't.'

She looked out of the car window; they were parked on a cobblestoned space before a large town house. She looked around her for a second time more carefully, and trying to gather woolly wits. She was sure she had been here before, or somewhere very like it. She said in a small, ashamed voice:

'I'm not sure…where are we, please?'

'Alkmaar.'

She turned round and looked at him properly then and said with palpable relief, 'Oh, so we haven't started.'

He smiled very nicely. 'On the contrary, we have had a pleasant drive round the country—Bergen, Schoorl, and then across the canal to Schagen and

Benningbroek, through Hoorn to Avenhorn. The country looked delightful and we didn't hurry.'

She was mortified to feel tears prick her eyes. She repeated, 'I'm so sorry,' and sniffed.

'Up all night, were you?' His voice was so kind that she had to fight the tears. 'I should have thought of that. Couldn't you bring yourself to tell me?'

She answered truthfully, 'No. It was so kind of you to take me out, and I thought I'd be able to stay awake. I—I was looking forward to it.' She had quite forgotten her annoyance.

'So was I,' he said briefly.

'You've wasted a whole afternoon. Why did you bother, with me snoring beside you?'

'But it wasn't wasted—you could have woken up at any moment.'

'Only I didn't. I've made a mess of your afternoon. I—I think I'd better go home.' She peered around her. 'I can't quite remember where we are, though I must have been past here.'

'Of course you're not going home, you silly girl. You're coming in to have tea.' He sounded as though he was laughing.

'Where?' She looked uncertainly at the lovely old red brick façade of the house before them. 'Not here?'

'Why not? It's my home.'

She said uncertainly, 'It's rather grand.'

He didn't laugh or even smile, but said simply, 'Is it? Perhaps—but it's home too and has been for generations of us. There's nothing grand about that, is there?'

'No. I'd like to come to tea, thank you.' She sat up straight. 'Do I look awful?'

He sighed and said gently, 'Oh, my dear Miss Augusta Brown...' and she said sharply, 'You always call me that. My name's Miss Brown, but mostly I get called Augusta—but never the way you say it, as though I were different.'

'But you are different.' He spoke lazily, with a little smile, so that she was sure that he was teasing.

He got out of the car and opened the door for her and they went together across the cobblestones and up the double steps and in through the great carved door with its handsome fanlight.

CHAPTER FOUR

THE HALL WAS exactly as Augusta had imagined it would be—black and white tiles underfoot; dark, panelled walls and a plaster ceiling of great beauty. The furniture was in keeping—there was an oak draw-table in its centre, its bulbous legs betraying its Flemish origin, and along one wall was a vast walnut cupboard, ornately carved and flanked by two chairs, which she recognised as Indo-Dutch; Burgomaster chairs in ebony and cushioned in blue velvet. Against the opposite wall was a carved oak wall table, decorated with a great deal of strap work and having a marble top upon which rested a vast Delft china soup tureen, filled with hyacinths. A large mirror, its gilded wood frame also carved, hung above it. The staircase was at the back of the hall, mounting to a half landing and then branching left and right to the floor above. All the furniture were museum pieces, but there was nothing of the museum in the atmosphere of the old house; it was warm and fragrant, and lived in. She turned to remark upon this to her host, but before she could do so, a shrill voice from somewhere upstairs cried, 'Papa, Papa!' and a small girl, perhaps four or five, came down the stairs at a great pace, to stop halfway and look at them and say, '*Dag...*' and then descend the remaining stairs quite slowly.

Dr van Lindemann went to meet her, swung her off her feet, kissed her soundly and said, 'Come and meet Miss Augusta Brown, Johanna.'

The moppet obediently offered a small hand, at the same time observing that she was delighted to make Miss Brown's acquaintance...and Augusta, not to be outdone, answered in a similar vein before being led through one of the doors in the hall. The room they entered was presumably the drawing room and very magnificent. The walls were covered in tapestries and the marble fireplace was flanked by gilded pillars, most elaborately carved. The plaster ceiling was as fine a one as that of the hall, and there was a thin, silky carpet covering most of the wooden floor. This much Augusta was able to see without actually staring, but her surroundings were not those to be taken in at a glance—she hoped that they would have tea there, so that she could look around her. In the meantime she had another more urgent problem. Who was the small creature dancing across the room to look out of the window? The doctor hadn't said, but she had called 'Papa' as she had come downstairs. The thought depressed Augusta, for although she had told herself many times that he was probably married, the concrete evidence of this was hard to accept. She would have to find out, for her interest in him was getting too great for her peace of mind. She was given the opportunity almost immediately, for the doctor, after ushering her to a chair, begged to be excused while he made an important telephone call. As soon as the door had closed behind him, she got up and wandered over to the window. It overlooked a fair-sized garden traditionally Dutch in its symmetrical neatness, and planted with row upon row of spring flowers. She exclaimed, 'Oh, how pretty!' and Johanna came a little nearer and looked up at her, and said with the engaging candour of extreme youth:

'I like you, though your hair's a funny colour.'

'Thank you, Johanna.' Augusta was careful not to smile. 'I think you're nice too.' And then, because she wanted to know so badly, 'Whose little girl are you?'

The small creature stared at her with round eyes. 'Papa's, of course,' she uttered succinctly.

'And Mama?' prompted Augusta gently, the better side of her nature aware that she wasn't behaving well—but she did want to know.

'Mama is in Paris.'

Augusta, staring at a bed of scarlet parrot tulips and not seeing them at all, remembered that Miss Susan Belsize was in Paris—and then dismissed the thought which followed it as absurd. But was it absurd? She had seen that the doctor and Susan Belsize had been on very good terms with each other—the easy, casual terms of long friendship, or husband and wife. Perhaps Miss Belsize was an actress and preferred to be known by her maiden name. It sounded silly, but silly things had a habit of not being so silly upon occasion. The longer she reflected upon it, the more feasible it seemed.

'You're not talking,' remarked a small accusing voice.

She made haste to remedy this. By the time Doctor van Lindemann returned, they were deep in lively discussion as to the exact dress Johanna intended to wear when she was grown up enough to be a bride.

Augusta found it a little difficult to meet the doctor's eye as they sat down. He had observed as he came in that tea would be coming at any minute, and she had gone back to her chair, to find that he had taken the chair opposite her—it was an eighteenth-century sleeping chair of some magnificence, but its comfort appeared to have little effect upon its occupant, who looked wide awake and likely to remain so. He said at once:

'What's the matter? You look as though you've just had bad news.'

It came as a shock to her to realise that it had been bad news. She had allowed him to loom large in her thoughts—a state of affairs she would have to correct immediately if she wasn't going to make a fool of herself.

She said now, sedately, 'Bad news? How could I possibly...?'

His pale gaze held hers. 'I've no idea at the moment—but I shall find out.' He smiled suddenly at her and then transferred his attention to Johanna, who had settled herself in a winged armchair by the window. He put out a long arm and pulled a small stool close to his own chair.

'Come and sit by me, Johanna—you'll make crumbs in that chair and then Jannie will tear us both limb from limb.'

As he spoke the door opened and a small round woman trotted in with the tea tray. She began, as she crossed the room, 'What nonsense you do talk, Doctor—to listen to you, one would think I was a tyrant!'

She chuckled richly at the very idea and he laughed with her, then looked at Augusta. 'This is my housekeeper and friend, Jannie... Miss Brown is staying with Juffrouw van den Pol, Jannie—a niece from England, but her Dutch is not bad—not bad at all.'

Augusta, who was proud of her command of that language, drew an indignant breath, but before she could speak, he went on, 'Be mother, will you, Augusta? It's something we lack at the moment!'

She wondered, as she poured tea from the bullet-shaped silver teapot, if he had been offering her an opening for her questions, and decided not. He wasn't a devious man—probably he had made the remark without thought. They drank their tea from Amstel china teacups, painted delicately with rural scenes, and ate paper-thin sandwiches and tiny cakes from matching plates. They talked about gardens and birds and animals, and Johanna joined in.

'Have you any animals?' she wanted to know of Augusta.

'Yes, three dogs, two cats and a donkey.' She and the child discussed Bottom at some length, while the doctor sat back in his chair, watching them.

They had almost finished tea when the door behind Augusta opened and Johanna jumped off her stool, her small face radiant. As she ran across the room she shouted 'Papa—Papa!' and Augusta, taken unawares, looked up, the expression on her face unguarded, to meet the doctor's eye. Her cheeks grew pink at the thought of the mistake she had so nearly made, and pinker still under his interested gaze. Before she could look away, his expression changed—he looked at her with narrowed eyes, and began to shake with laughter.

'Well, I'll be damned! So that was the bad news... And you don't have to look so guilty. After all, I was only conforming very nicely to the character you have seen fit to saddle me with, was I not? What a pity it is that I cannot live up to your lively imagination, my dear Augusta. I can admit only to being Johanna's uncle—and despite your worst fears, she has a mother who is legally and very happily married to my brother.'

Augusta sat speechless, uncertain as to whether he was amused or hiding annoyance; it was fortunate that Johanna and her father joined them and she looked up to see a man very like the doctor, but younger and not quite as tall or broad, but his hair was the same pale straw and his eyes as light a blue. The doctor had got out of his chair.

'Hullo, Huib. Augusta, this is my brother, staying with me at the moment. Huib, this is Miss Augusta Brown, from England, a niece of Juffrouw van den Pol.'

She shook hands, and Huib said cheerfully, 'How nice to meet you. I've been wanting to improve my English.'

They both laughed, and Jannie came in with fresh tea and they all sat down again, until she glanced at the bracket clock on the wall table by her chair and saw that it was almost five o'clock, and sprang to her feet.

'I had no idea it was late—I'm sorry, but I really have to go—my aunts...' She babbled a little, anxious to get away and yet afraid that her haste might appear ill-mannered.

The doctor had got up too. 'You can be home in five minutes,' he remarked mildly. 'The car's outside.'

'Oh no. Please don't bother—it's quite close by, isn't it? I...'

She was interrupted with a faint impatience. 'I have to pay an evening visit to your aunt...you might just as well come in the car, although if you prefer to walk...?'

He was laughing at her behind the placid look. Her green eyes snapped. She said with dignity, 'Thank you. I shall be glad of a lift.'

She bade Johanna goodbye, taking care not to hope that she might see her again, for fear the doctor might think she was angling for another visit; certainly he made no mention of her doing so as they went to the car. They drove the short distance in silence, and had still not spoken when they entered her aunts' house together. There was no one about—though a vague murmur of voices from the kitchen indicated that Tante Emma and Mevrouw Blom were doing something about supper—Maartje would be with Tante Marijna. Augusta turned to go upstairs and was restrained by a hand on her arm. A pity, for she had just reached the conclusion that the least said about the deplorable afternoon the better; now, whatever he had to say, she would feel constrained to apologise once more. She stopped reluctantly, and he said in a placid voice:

'You always rush away...I can't think how Archie keeps up with you.'

She looked at him in utter bewilderment. 'How did you know about Archie?' she managed at length.

He stood looking at her, considering her question. 'I was at Edinburgh with Weller-Pratt, he's one of his housemen.'

It explained a lot. 'You asked me about Lady Belway going home and wanted to know...' she paused, then went on with some asperity:

'You didn't want to know at all—you only had to ask Mr Weller-Pratt if you know him as well as all that.'

He agreed with her in the friendliest possible manner, which enraged her. She had her mouth open to ask him why he had bothered to ask her anyway, thought better of it, and closed it with something of a snap.

'That's right,' he said, still very friendly. 'Don't ask, because I'm not sure that I'm ready to answer you.' He smiled in such a way that her heart turned over with a lurch which she told herself was due to her extreme tiredness.

'Do you believe in fate?' His voice was quiet, compelling too.

She was cross—it was a silly conversation—she hadn't understood his last remark, and the rest had been disappointing, why, she refused to admit, even to herself. She said with asperity, 'I suppose so,' and saw that for some reason, he was amused. 'How grudging—but at least we agree about something. Shall we go up?'

Tante Marijna had had a restful afternoon; she was delighted to see them and ready for a gossip. She had to wait, of course, until the doctor had examined her, pronounced satisfaction at her progress, and given Augusta further instructions. These duties performed, however, he disposed himself in a chair and prepared to indulge his patient.

Augusta, once he no longer required her services, had gone to her room where she took stock of her face and hair, taking rather longer than she need have done. She didn't particularly want to go down to her aunt's room while the doctor was still there, but it smacked of cowardice if she didn't...sooner or later Tante Marijna would have to know that she had spent the afternoon sleeping instead of being a pleasant companion to Dr van Lindemann. She didn't think he was the kind of man to tell tales, even for a laugh; it would be left to her. She went downstairs again, slowly. They were chatting about Johanna and as she went in, he said easily, bringing her into the conversation, 'You got on rather well with her, didn't you, Augusta? She can be difficult sometimes, and of course a nurse can't take the place of her mother, however good she is—she adores Huib.'

He looked directly at Augusta, who had gone to sit in a small Victorian lady's chair on the other side of her aunt's bed. 'Your aunt wanted to know what you thought of the country, Augusta.'

So he hadn't told. She swallowed and plunged without preamble:

'I went to sleep—the whole time.' She could see the look on Tante Marijna's face. 'It was unpardonable of me, but Doctor van Lindemann was—was kind enough not to mind. I woke up in time for tea,' she added hopefully, with much the same air as that of a bad bridge player producing a trump card.

Her aunt said in a reproachful whisper, 'Augusta, how could you?' to be interrupted by the doctor. 'I'm the one to blame, Juffrouw van den Pol, Augusta was up for a good deal of the night before last, and for the whole of last night as well. She was asleep on her feet, and I blame myself that I didn't see it. However, you are so much better, I think that she might sleep in a room close by tonight, just in case you need her. She would have stayed with you whatever you had said last night, you know, so don't worry on that score. I'm hoping that she will forgive me enough to allow me to take her out again.'

Augusta met his bland stare. She had no intention of going out with him again; she flashed him a look with her green eyes which told him so and which he countered smoothly by saying to her aunt, 'The day after tomorrow—I shall have a free afternoon. A little fresh air is good for her, I think—I'm sure the same arrangement could be made.'

She watched her aunt agree with him, and when they both looked at her, smiling, she smiled herself, unwillingly, because there was really nothing else to do. 'There now,' said Tante Marijna with satisfaction, 'won't that be nice? Take Constantijn down to the door, will you, Augusta?'

Augusta got up reluctantly. 'Maartje's in the kitchen—she will hear Dr van Lindemann on the stairs—you wouldn't mind, Doctor? There are some things to do for Aunt.'

It was no use; he said to infuriate her, 'Of course I mind—besides, there's something I forgot to tell you.'

She went to the door without a word. After all, it might be something important about Tante Marijna which he didn't want the old lady to hear. Whatever it was, however, he kept to himself as they went down to the house door, so that she felt forced to ask, 'You wanted to tell me something, Doctor?'

He opened the door. 'Ah, yes, my dear Miss Brown. You don't snore.'

He didn't come until almost eleven o'clock the next morning, by which time, Augusta, thoroughly rested, and having had time to have a good think, had reached the conclusion that she had behaved rather stupidly. She must have given him considerable amusement, for if all his girl-friends—and her vivid imagination had allowed him at least half a dozen—

were like Susan Belsize, she herself must have appeared incredibly homespun. Probably he was bored, and because she was a new face, even if not a pretty one, he was indulging in a little mild dalliance in order to pass the time until he could see the luscious Susan once again. It was a lowering thought and a depressing one too, but once she got back to St Jude's, she would forget all about him—after all, there would be Archie. She frowned, because Archie had in all probability found another girl to take to the cinema. Her frown deepened when she realised that she really didn't care in the least if he had.

She was careful to be very polite to the doctor when he called, saying 'Yes, Doctor, no, Doctor' with such meekness that when she saw him out he turned on the stairs with a suddenness which caused her to run full tilt into his waistcoat, and exploded, 'Good God, girl! What on earth's the matter with you? I've never known you so mealy-mouthed...don't you feel well?'

She was at once indignant. 'Well?... Of course I'm well. I'm being polite and—and professional, that's all.'

He stared at her through narrowed lids, so that she could barely see his eyes' pale gleam. 'Now why in the name of thunder should you suddenly wish to be that? You've had time to think, of course, and you've probably tied a dozen ideas into a knot no man can hope to unravel.'

His voice became suddenly and unexpectedly gentle. 'Look, dear Augusta Brown, it's really quite simple. We met in England—hardly friends, should I say, but at least we met. And now we meet again. What is more natural than us seeing more of each other while you are here? We do no harm to Archie—or anyone else.' He sighed. 'You're rather a goose.'

He bent his head and kissed her lightly upon one cheek, and then ran lightly down the remainder of the stairs and let himself out, leaving her standing alone, feeling foolish.

He had apparently forgotten all about it by the evening, for when he came to see Tante Marijna, he made a few casual references to the weather—and these delivered with the air of a man wishing to be civil and no more. Augusta was disappointed and vaguely annoyed. She toyed with the idea of declining his invitation for the following day, and decided against this, telling herself that if she did so, she would never find out anything about him. She didn't know much as it was, and she was unlikely to set eyes on him again once she was back in London; which fact she rather illogically considered sufficient reason for finding out as much as possible while she had the chance.

When he came the following morning, it was to say, as he went again, that there was no reason for him to come in that evening. 'Your aunt is going along well—I'll be in tomorrow just before noon—and mind and be ready for me.'

Augusta bristled. 'I'm always ready—when have you ever found your patient not...'

'I said "you",' he interposed placidly. 'I thought we could go somewhere and lunch.'

She blushed faintly—it was vexing the number of times he put her, in the nicest possible way, in the wrong. 'Oh, well. That would be nice. I'll arrange something with Maartje.'

'I've already done that. When do you return to England?'

She answered with something like surprise, because she hadn't thought about it. 'In four days' time. Have you been able to do anything about a nurse—I'm afraid I must go back.'

He shot her a glance which she didn't understand at all—speculation—calculation, even. She wondered about it. He, being a doctor, must know that she had very little choice in the matter—it wasn't as if she worked in an office and could telephone to say that she wouldn't be coming back for a day or two and could they manage.

He said slowly, 'Ah, yes, of course. Private Patients again, or will you be going back to Men's Surgical? You didn't like PP, did you?'

'No. Although I liked some of the patients. The Brig and Lady Belway, though she was a tyr...' She stopped. 'I'm sorry—I forgot she was your godmother.'

'And as you were about to say—a tyrant. You're right, of course, but she's a lonely old woman, too. She liked you.'

'I can't think why. I went and had tea with her before I came on holiday.'

He smiled. 'Yes, I know. She wrote and told me so. I won't tell you exactly what she said, for I don't think we know each other well enough.' He had been lounging against the wall, now he picked up his bag. 'I've a couple more visits. Let me know if you're at all worried.'

He nodded briskly at her and opened the door, and she stood holding it while he got into the Mini and drove away.

The following day it rained. Not a gentle spring rain, but a steady drizzle, blown hither and thither by a cool wind from off the North Sea. Augusta, who had planned what she should wear down to the last pin, realised that the only suitable attire would be a raincoat and a headscarf. She had both with her—but she had counted on wearing the outfit she had travelled over in. She looked out of the windows at least a dozen times before midday, and by half past eleven it was obvious that the rain had come to stay. Perhaps he would put the whole thing off; travelling around Holland on a very wet day was hardly enjoyable unless you were with someone so interesting that the weather went unnoticed. She was forced to admit to herself that, as far as she was concerned, the weather would be unnoticed, but she didn't think he would feel the same. She had only to think of Susan Belsize to be sure of that.

She did all she had to do for her aunt, and then went to find Tante Emma and Maartje, to make sure that everything was going smoothly. Mevrouw Blom had just returned from a shopping expedition—the sight of her, dripping water from a plastic mac, and with wisps of damp hair hanging forlornly from her headscarf, was almost more than Augusta could bear. She went back upstairs, and to distract her thoughts, read a large slice of the day's news to Tante Marijna, until she at last heard the doctor's tread on the stairs.

It was almost noon, but he appeared in no hurry to go. He examined his patient, and then sat down by the bedside for five minutes or so, talking trivialities. Augusta, on the other side of the bed, had to make an effort not to fidget, which resulted in her sitting as though carved in stone. Presently, he caught her eye. 'Ready?' he asked casually, and as she stood up: 'That's a pretty dress. It suits you.'

She remembered that she had told him about Pieter—perhaps he was just being polite, but he continued, laughing, 'No, I'm not buttering you up. I mean it.'

She bit her lip. He really was a most provoking man, and quite the most interesting one she had ever met... She smiled suddenly at him.

'Two minutes,' she said.

The Rolls was outside. She had expected the Mini, and said so, but as they got in, he observed, 'The Mini's fine for me, but I rather feel that I get the lion's share once I'm in, which is rather hard on my passenger. Besides, this car's so much more comfortable should you wish to take a nap.' He flashed her a quizzical, wholly friendly smile, and she smiled back, completely at ease. 'Where are we going?' she wanted to know.

'Since the weather's against us, I thought Amsterdam—we can lunch there, and if you want to do any shopping, presents and so forth, we could do that in the afternoon. Mevrouw Blom is staying until six o'clock, so we shall have plenty of time to follow our inclination.'

They had gone smoothly through the town and were out on the Amsterdam road, but not the motorway. It was a smaller, secondary road beside the canal, which took them through Akersloot and then alongside the Alkmaarder Meer. They stopped for a few minutes to look at the water, grey under a grey sky, and whipped into fussy little waves by the wind. There were no yachts to be seen, and it all looked a little dreary, but Augusta, who wasn't feeling in the least dreary, entered into a lively discussion about sailing with the doctor, and when he stopped her in the middle of a sentence and said impatiently, 'Oh, do for heaven's sake call me Constantijn,' she said, 'Yes, all right,' and went on making her point about sailing dinghies. She was enjoying herself very much; after all this was the first time she had been out with him, for she refused to count the sleep she had had in his car as an outing, and they hadn't talked much over tea. He was, she quickly discovered, amusing and excellent company, and unlike Pieter he hadn't mentioned himself once. Which reminded her; she still had to find out about Susan Belsize, and whether he went to London very often, and if so, why. She did her best to bring the conversation round to this interesting point, but somehow it wasn't easy—it was almost as if he knew what she was trying to do, and was deliberately hindering her. They were nearing the outskirts of Amsterdam, and she was no nearer knowing. She gave up, for the moment at any rate, and allowed herself to enjoy to the full what was undoubtedly going to be a delightful day, whatever the weather.

She wondered about parking the car as they drove deeper into the heart of the city, but she need not have worried, for Constantijn had chosen to lunch at the Excelsior, which was in the Hotel de l'Europe anyway, and the hotel had a garage. She arranged to meet him in the bar and went away to repair the ravages of the journey. The raincoat and scarf disposed of, she looked passably well turned out, even for the Excelsior, and if she hadn't been fairly certain of this, his open admiration would have convinced her. He ordered their drinks and observed:

'You wore those shoes with a green dress. The sun

was shining—you looked like...' he paused. 'You didn't belong to London at all.'

She sipped her Dubonnet. 'Well, I don't,' she said matter-of-factly. 'I was born in Dorset, and though I don't live at home any more, that doesn't mean to say I shouldn't like to.'

'Then why don't you?' He smiled at her, his pale eyes deepened and warmed with sympathy.

'Well, how can I?' she wanted to know. 'I—I must earn my living and there aren't any large hospitals near my home—even the small ones are too far away for me to live out. No, it has to be London, I'm afraid. I can get home once a month at least, and there's more chance of getting on.'

'A Sister's post? I simply can't imagine you—Oh, I don't mean you aren't capable—quite obviously you are. What about Archie?'

She stared into her glass, then took out the cherry and ate it before replying. 'You keep on about Archie,' she said at length.

'Twice,' he replied smoothly, 'and only because we—Lady Belway and Sue and myself—decided that you were far too alive to stay in hospital for the rest of your life. Archie seemed the answer.'

She said flatly, 'Well, he's not. Discussing me behind my back...' her eyes flashed, which for some reason gave a glow to her rusty hair.

'Naturally,' he said imperturbably. 'Didn't you ever discuss us?'

She went pink under his gently mocking gaze. 'Yes—at least, it was mostly Miss Belsize's clothes.'

She was unprepared for his deep bellow of laughter. 'I deserved that. But of course, Sue's clothes are—er—outstanding.'

It was the chance she had been waiting for. She began 'Who...?' and he deprived her neatly of it. 'If we're going to bicker, let's do it over a meal—it's so much more comfortable and I'm famished. I was up most of the night with a baby case, and by the time I got back, it was time for morning surgery.'

She said instantly, her mouth curved in sympathy, 'Oh, how awful for you! Why didn't you say so—I could have made coffee for you before we left...' She broke off, conscious that her concern had sounded rather warmer than need be. He didn't seem to have noticed. He said mildly:

'Nice of you to say so, but it would have delayed our trip, wouldn't it, and I've been looking forward to it.' He went on deliberately, 'And you? Have you been looking forward to it too?'

Without hesitation she answered, 'Oh, yes.' And then, 'You shouldn't shoot questions at me like that. I didn't have time to prevar...' she frowned, 'tell fibs,' she ended.

He began to laugh. 'The word is prevaricate. And do you find it necessary to—er—tell fibs to me? If so, you really shouldn't.'

'It's of no use anyway, I'm no good at it—social fibbing, I mean. I tell just as many as everyone else, but people always know.'

They had sat down at their table; he picked up his menu and began to study it. Without looking up he said, 'Well, I should warn you never to try it on me, for I should most certainly know. Now, what would you like to eat? How about mushrooms in cream and sherry for a starter and then the terrine of duck—and I see that there's that delicious pudding, Marquise Montmorency, which I can recommend.'

Augusta agreed happily; she had had her fair share of going out, but rarely on this level. In a way, it seemed a waste of good food, for she was enjoying his company so much that she would have been just as happy with a cup of coffee and a plate of sandwiches. But when the food came she was forced to admit to herself that it was perfection and made more so by the right companion with which to eat it, and spiced with a conversation which never once flagged. They talked about everything under the sun, and she was much struck by the discovery that they agreed closely about everything that mattered most. It was vaguely disquieting, too, to find herself telling him some of her deeper thoughts and feelings. She stopped in mid-sentence, much struck by this fact, her green eyes wide. He said quietly:

'You agreed with me that you believe in Fate...sometimes two people meet, you know. Perhaps only for a brief hour, sometimes for a lifetime, sharing the same star.'

Augusta stared at him. 'How did you know what I was thinking?' she asked breathlessly, because he had put into words something that had lain at the back of her mind like the shreds of a dream.

He lifted an eyebrow. 'My dear Miss Augusta Brown, your face is like an open book for me to read.' He smiled a little, his eyes twinkling, so that she was emboldened to ask, 'Why did you ask me if my thumbs pricked?'

The smile became mocking. 'What? Is your knowledge of Shakespeare so poor? I can't believe that.'

'Of course it's not,' she said crossly. 'But you're— you're not something wicked...'

'From the way you treated me, very off-hand and hoity-toity, I rather gathered that I was.'

She giggled; wrinkling her tip-tilted nose in an engaging manner which was all the more engaging because she was unaware of it, and paused to watch the waiter as he served their pudding. It was a glorious confection of meringue and cherries, chocolate cream and whipped cream, adorned with little cornets lined with chocolate and themselves bulging with cream. It tasted even better than it looked. She savoured the last mouthful of it and Constantijn asked:

'Want some more, Augusta? No? Coffee, then?'

They sat over it, still talking, this time more light-heartedly, telling each other about their childhood. He asked abruptly, 'Where exactly do you live?'

She didn't intend to tell him. It was unlikely that he knew England all that well, and Dorset was still very rural. She was vague.

'On the border of Dorset and Somerset...I thought I had told you. Between two villages, miles from anywhere. It's entirely different from London. Do you like London?'

His good manners would not allow him to ignore her evasion. They talked about the theatres and discussed the parks and how delightful it was to ride on top of a bus through London, but never once did he mention Susan Belsize.

It was still raining when they decided to walk around and look at the shops. Augusta was surprised—most men loathed looking in shop windows. She said so, and he replied:

'I couldn't agree more, but it does rather depend on who you are with, you know.'

They strolled along, getting soaked without noticing it at all, stopping to gaze at anything which caught their eye, and presently they turned away from the main streets and wandered off down the small, old streets lining the canals. Their waters looked dull and sluggish, the trees which lined their banks dripped steadily, even the old houses with their picturesque steeple roofs looked damp and sad. They stood in the middle of a little bridge spanning the water, and looked around them.

'It's beautiful,' said Augusta, and meant it. 'Water mains and electricity and cars haven't made any difference, have they? It still belongs to its own time.'

Constantijn leaned his elbows on the bridge's stone balustrade.

'You like Holland.' It was a statement, not a question, but she answered it at once. 'Yes—very much. You see, I've visited the aunts regularly for as long as I can remember. I used to sit on Tante Emma's knee while she read Sjors to me.'

They smiled at each other, sharing a remembered pleasure from their childhood. Constantijn said presently, 'He goes on for ever and ever—just like Rupert Bear in England. You can still buy the book—a bit updated, of course. Johanna adores him—so did I.' He laughed. 'I suppose every child in Holland has had Sjors read to him at bedtime.'

Augusta was watching a horse and cart trundling slowly down the street, its driver stopping at each doorway to collect the food scraps each householder had left tidily in a bin for the pigs. When the doctor asked:

'Would you like to live in Holland, Augusta?' she answered him without taking her eyes off the slow-moving cart:

'You mean for ever and ever? I wouldn't mind at all. Only I'd want to go to England for holidays. I did think about it when I qualified last year, but it means doing a year over here as a student to get a Dutch qualification before I could stay as a trained nurse indefinitely...and I've still got my Midwifery to do, and perhaps Children's. They'll take up a couple of years at least.'

She turned to look at him, and found him smiling a little. 'Ah, of course, I had forgotten your career.' He stood up and said abruptly:

'Would you rather have tea here or go back to Alkmaar and have it with Johanna?'

She chose the latter, because she dearly wanted to see his home again—besides that, she wanted a breathing space. She had been in his company for only a few hours; and she was fast losing her common sense, owing, no doubt, to the fact that they had been flung into each other's company during the last week and there was nothing much else to interest her in Alkmaar. She told herself with firmness, so that she would believe it.

The rain took on a fresh fury as the doctor turned the car's nose towards Alkmaar. Nevertheless, he said lightly:

'Since we're out for pleasure, I thought we'd go back through Velsen and along the coast road. You know, through Castricum and Egmond-Binnen. The dunes will be sodden...we haven't been lucky with the weather, have we?'

They talked all the way home, and when they reached Alkmaar, Augusta admitted to herself that she hadn't noticed the dunes at all, because she had been thinking exclusively of the man beside her, even while she carried on an intelligent conversation with him.

It was pleasant to go indoors, into the faint warmth of the old house. They were met in the hall by Johanna, who shrieked with pleasure because they had come back in time for tea, and then, obedient to her uncle's request, led Augusta upstairs to comb her hair and repair her complexion.

The little girl took her to a bedroom on the first floor—a large room furnished simply and perfectly with a canopied bed, hung with the same patterned chintz as the curtains, and an enormous pillow cupboard against one wall. The other wall held a fireplace with a burnished steel grate and embellished with a quantity of carved wood. There was a Pembroke table between the two windows, holding a round mirror and a quantity of silver; and a number of comfortable chairs. Augusta sat down before the mirror and took the pins out of her hair, while Johanna perched on the side of the bed, watching her.

'Your hair's a nice colour,' she observed at length.

Augusta smiled, and said, 'Is this your room, Johanna? It's very beautiful.'

'No—my room's along the passage and up the stairs—Nurse sleeps up there too. Susan slept here,' she added, to shatter Augusta's quiet thoughts, and cause her to dig a pin into her scalp and wince with pain. 'Oh, yes, Susan Belsize,' she answered in as careless a voice as she could muster. 'I met her in London. Isn't she pretty?'

The small creature nodded vigorously. 'Uncle Constantijn says she's just too gorgeous, but Papa doesn't say that, because Mama's much prettier.' She got off the bed and came close to Augusta and peered into her face. 'You're not pretty exactly,' she remarked, and added kindly, 'But you've got green eyes.'

They went downstairs again presently, to find the doctor in the drawing room, standing in front of the small open fire. His gaze swept over them both and returned to Augusta. She jumped visibly when he asked:

'And what has my small niece been telling you this time?'

Before she could reply, Johanna shrilled, 'We talked about the bedroom. I told Augusta that Susan sleeps in it when she comes.'

She pranced across the room to him. 'Your Susan, Uncle Constantijn, your gorgeous Susan with the black hair,' she chanted.

He picked her up and tossed her high into the air, and she shrieked with delight. As he put her down he said easily:

'Sit down, Augusta. Tea will be here in a minute. Come over here by the fire—it's not cold, but it's cheerful after all that grey sky.'

He sat down opposite her, and started to tell her about the nurse he had found for Tante Marijna, and she realised that, for some reason or other, nothing more was going to be said about the lovely Miss Belsize. She was, she discovered, boiling with rage; the fun had gone out of the day; she fought a strong desire to get up and walk out of the house, only that wouldn't be very practical, as her raincoat and scarf had been borne away to be dried, and the rain was coming down harder than ever. It was fortunate that Huib came in at that moment and there was little need to talk very much to Constantijn. She ate her tea without appetite and got up to go soon afterwards. By then her rage had evaporated, leaving nothing but a rather sad feeling that she was just what Susan had said—a ship passing in the night, someone to whom it was unnecessary to explain things, even though for a few hours at least, she and Constantijn had reached a depth of friendship she would not have believed possible. All the same, he had no intention of allowing her to know anything of himself or his life, however pleasant their relationship had been a short time ago.

She stood making conversation, while he went to fetch her things, and when he returned, she tied the scarf rather savagely with no regard at all for her appearance and buttoned her raincoat with quick determined fingers. She said goodbye to Huib, whom she liked, to Johanna who demanded a prolonged hug, and went briskly to the door, followed by Constantijn, to whom she kept up a constant flow of meaningless chatter, partly because she was nervous, and partly because it kept her from thinking. Outside the drawing room door, he took her arm and drew her in the opposite direction to the front door.

'There's a rather interesting room you should see,' he remarked conversationally, cutting through her babble as though he hadn't heard a word of it. 'Painted—done by the same man who did the Town Hall in Dokkum. I should like you to see it.'

He was leading her across the hall as he spoke, taking no notice of her protests. Now he opened a small door under the right wing of the staircase and led her inside. It was indeed a beautiful room, although small. Its walls were canvas, painted with Biblical scenes, and it was simply, almost austerely furnished with an oak gatelegged table and some narrow rush-seated chairs. There were two carved oak arm-

chairs on either side of the tiled fireplace, and a corner
cupboard, upon the shelves of which was displayed a
collection of silver tankards. Augusta was interested
despite her firm intention not to be. She walked to
the centre of the room, and ran an appreciative hand
over the mellow, shining wood of the table top. 'It's
like a Pieter de Hooch painting,' she murmured, and
went to peer at the tankards. They were all different,
and all, she judged, sixteenth or seventeenth century.
She turned round to ask about them, and perceived
that the doctor had shut the door, and was lounging
against it, staring at her. He looked forbidding and a
little arrogant. He said forcefully:

'You are the most stubborn girl! I had hoped this
afternoon... But no, you are determined to make me
into the villain of your imagination. I thought that you
might change your mind when you got to know me
a little, but I see that it is useless.' He sighed loudly,
took a couple of strides across the little room, and
caught her by the shoulders, not at all gently. He said,
in quite a temper, 'Well, my pretty—if you want a
villain, how's this for a start?'

No one had ever kissed her like that before. It took
her breath and emptied her head of sense and set her
heart thudding. When he let her go, she stood, with
his hands still on her shoulders, and stared at him with
huge green eyes shining with the tears she had no
intention of shedding—not in front of him anyway.

'I'm too angry to think of anything to say,' she said
icily, 'but when I do I shall say it.' Her voice wobbled
a little and she closed her mouth tightly because it
was shaking. He said nothing at all, and when she
stole a look at him, it was disconcerting to find that
he didn't appear in the least ashamed of himself. In-

stead, he stood aside for her to pass and opened the
door for her, before walking beside her to the front
door. They didn't speak at all on the short drive, but
as she got out of the car at her aunts' door, she contrived to say in a normal voice, 'Do you want to see
my aunt, Doctor?'

He already had his door open. 'Of course I do. But
don't worry, Miss Augusta Brown, I never combine
business with pleasure—you'll be quite safe.'

Augusta tossed her head with such violence that a
pin fell out, and a tiresome tress of hair fell over her
face. When he laughed softly, she could have cheerfully thrown something at him, but there was nothing
handy—only a valuable porcelain vase on the hall
table.

CHAPTER FIVE

IT WAS a pity that the doctor didn't find it necessary to pay her aunt a visit the following day, for Augusta had several wakeful hours, rehearsing a selection of remarks suitable for his reception. They varied greatly, from something short and scathing, through the whole gamut of emotions, to a gentle reproof, very dignified and forgiving. She rather thought that she would choose that one, and finally went to sleep, pleased with her efforts, only to wake an hour or so later, and recall with clarity the regrettable incident in the painted room, so that she changed her mind once more. It was getting light by the time she went to sleep again, and that only after admitting to herself that she hadn't minded being kissed roughly by Constantijn in the very least; what she had minded, though, was that he had done it to annoy her.

He didn't come until the evening of the following day, by which time Augusta's frustration had rendered her alternatively icy with ill-temper or acutely miserable because she might not see him again—a natural enough feeling, she told herself, as she would have no opportunity of paying him back in his own ill-mannered coin. She reminded herself of this repeatedly throughout a long and tedious day, and as the evening approached and there was still no sign of him, declared to herself that she was delighted not to be seeing him again, a view wholly at variance with the interest she showed in any passing car.

And when he did come, he wasn't alone. He brought the nurse with him—Zuster Wils, a round-faced, blue-eyed creature who obviously adored him. He greeted Augusta with a cheerful friendliness which she hadn't reckoned with, so that she was prevented, most effectively, from making any of the speeches she had so painstakingly thought up. She remained silent while the arrangements for Tante Marijna's care were discussed, scowling at Zuster Wils' unsuspecting back, studying her covertly as she stood by Tante Marijna's bed, and forced to admit that the girl was pretty—blue eyes, honey-coloured hair and a way of looking up at the doctor through her lashes. Stupid creature, thought Augusta waspishly, and looked away to encounter Constantijn's hooded gaze, his mouth lifted by the faintest smile. She scowled at him too.

The visit was over in ten minutes—his large, cool hand engulfed hers for a brief moment while he made some polite comment on her journey home, and before she could think of a word to say, he had gone without so much as a backward glance.

It was pleasant to be home again, even if it were only for a couple of days. Charles had met her at Liverpool Street and had driven her down to Dorset in the Morris; its slightly elderly ways put her in mind of the effortless power and comfort of the Rolls-Royce, but she refused to allow herself the luxury of thinking about it or its owner. It had been an episode, nothing more. She told herself, for the hundredth time, that she didn't care if she never saw him again.

She made but the barest mention of him to her family; indeed, the portrait she painted of him was such as to leave them with the impression that he was

middle-aged, dull, and nothing much to look at, even
though she praised him highly as a doctor. In any case
there was so much to talk about, it was unnecessary
to do more than touch upon him from time to time.
She went back to St Jude's, well satisfied that she had
buried him so successfully in the back of her mind,
that she would never need to think of him again. It
was therefore disturbing to find an enormous cello-
phane-wrapped bouquet of tulips lying on her bed
when she got back to hospital. They were a rusty
bronze, with long delicate stems and leaves. She
opened the envelope tucked in among them and read.

'A subtle way of apologising for calling you carroty. These are called Bronze Queen.' It was signed,
rather coldly, she thought, C. van Lindemann. She
arranged them, in a collection of borrowed jugs and
vases, telling herself that he was merely doing what
any other man might do in similar circumstances, although she conceded that he need not have been quite
so lavish, and went down to her supper.

She was back on Men's Surgical in the morning
after a hasty breakfast—hasty because she had quite
forgotten to make up a clean cap the previous evening. The Sisters and staff nurses at St Jude's still
wore their old-fashioned starched and goffered caps,
of which they were immensely proud, despite the precious time they took to pleat and pin; they wore
strings too—small stiff bows under their chins, and
they had to be made up as well. Wrestling with them
long after she should have been in the dining room,
Augusta told herself crossly that it was Constantijn's
fault for sending her the tulips to distract her thoughts.
Their presence in her room had been the reason for
much comment among her friends, and her temper

had not been improved by one of them remarking at the table, as she swallowed tepid tea and bolted her buttered toast, that it was a good thing that she had such an attentive boy-friend, for Archie had been seen on several occasions with Mary Wilkes, Cas staff nurse. Mary, who had days off, wasn't there to substantiate this claim, although there was a murmur of agreement from everyone else present, cut short by the usual last-minute rush to get on the wards.

Most of the patients she had known had gone home, but there were still what Sister called the Hard Core—old Mr Reeves with diverticulitis, never quite well enough for operation; and the only time they had managed to get him up to the required standard of health to go to theatre, he had acquired a heavy cold and the anaesthetist had rejected him. Bill was still there too. He had been admitted as an acute peritonitis and had developed a paralytic ileus two or three days after his operation, and had been on a continuous stomach drainage and intravenous drip ever since— there could have been a further operation, but he was young and strong and wasn't in the least depressed by the monotonous regular treatment he had needed. Now after almost five weeks, he was recovering. Old Tom was there too; he had had a nephrolithotomy done, the stony results of which he proudly displayed in a little glass bottle on his locker. He was an old man, with no family life that anyone could discover, and now that he had developed a secondary infection, it was probably certain that he would stay where he was. He seemed content enough, and the nurses did their best to pander to his small simple wants. He had become a kind of legend on the ward, so that new patients were told about him and took their turn in reading the paper to him and seeing that he always got a cup of tea when there was one going.

The ward was full; but it always was, and Augusta was glad to be kept busy. She saw Archie within an hour or so of going on duty—they greeted each other with their usual friendliness, and over a lumbar puncture carried on a disjointed conversation, during which he told her without embarrassment that he had taken Mary Wilkes out on a number of occasions.

'I know,' said Augusta without rancour, 'I was told—someone always tells, don't they? Mary's great fun, and I'm not in the least jealous, Archie, just in case you're feeling guilty—though I'm sure you're not.'

They laughed together, and laughed again when he asked her if she would be prepared to go out with him when Mary wasn't off duty.

'No,' said Augusta, roundly. 'I wouldn't be so mean—Mary's much too nice. Anyway, I need all my free time so's I can find myself a millionaire.'

He had gone away in high good humour, and she hadn't really minded, although she had been joking about the millionaire. For the moment, at any rate, she had no interest whatsoever in marrying anyone.

The busy days slipped by, it seemed as though she had never been away and Alkmaar seemed part of a remote dream world. She busied herself writing letters to the great-aunts in her rather careless Dutch, and then, because it was May and warm and sunny, she played tennis; something she did quite well. She went swimming in the Serpentine too, which she did even better. She had a long weekend due to her in ten days' time; she would go home and potter for four days, gardening and helping her father with the animals.

She would lie about and do nothing too, and perhaps stroll around the country. The thought of it kept her happy, although the ten days seemed interminable. In the end, when she came off duty at five o'clock on the day before she had planned to go, she decided to travel down that evening because it had turned even warmer and the thought of sleeping in her own airy room at home was very tempting. She telephoned her mother, flung some things in an overnight bag, and caught the next train.

It was still light when she got out at Sherborne. Her father was waiting for her with the Mondeo estate and she got into the car beside him with such a sigh of relief that he asked her what was wrong.

'Nothing at all,' she protested, 'only it's so nice to be home again. London's awful—I mean the London I see. The parks are marvellous; I've been swimming, but there's never enough time to just lie about.'

She gazed appreciatively at the little town as they passed through it. It was, outwardly at least, asleep in the early summer twilight, and once they had turned off the main road there was nothing—no cars, no buses, no people pushing and jostling. She said on an impulse:

'I think I must get another job.'

Her father turned the car in through the open gateway. 'Restless, Roly?' He gave her a quick glance. 'That's not like you.'

She smiled at him. 'I've not settled down after my holiday, I suppose.'

She got out of the car and ran into the house and her mother took one look at her shadowed face and said, 'Hullo, darling. Supper, then bed—you're tired. You shall sleep round the clock.'

But Augusta awoke by seven the next morning, partly from habit and partly because she had been roused by the country sounds—birds, dogs barking, a sick horse whinnying in one of the loose boxes, and Bottom braying a morning greeting against the steady monotony of the cuckoos. The sun was pouring into her room too; she lay and watched it contentedly, then got up and went downstairs and joined everyone else for breakfast, for it was far too lovely a day to stay in bed. Presently she went back upstairs and put on slacks and a cotton shirt and tied her hair back with a green ribbon, then went to help with the chores, done without haste and made pleasant by the gentle gossip she and her mother enjoyed as they made beds and Hoovered and dusted. Mrs Crisp, the daily treasure, called them after a while, and they sat comfortably round the kitchen table, drinking the tea she had made because she could not abide coffee, and discussing the jumble sale which was to take place the next day. It was a yearly event of some importance locally—everyone went, everyone took something and bought something, so that it was a tremendous success financially, and an excellent opportunity to meet one's friends and have a chat. It was to be opened by some famous Army man, said her mother—his name had slipped her memory, but he had promised months previously. Something to do with the British Legion, she added, as though that fact made everything clear.

There wasn't anything to do after lunch; Mrs Crisp washed up and went home. Mrs Brown settled in a chair in the garden with what she told her daughter was an interesting novel; obviously a mistake, for within ten minutes she was quietly and soundly asleep. Her father and Charles had gone over to a neighbouring farm to perform a minor operation on a horse. Augusta read the paper, took some carrots to Bottom, and then, leaving the dogs with her sleeping parent, strolled off.

It was really very warm; she left the lane presently and struck off across the fields towards the woods skirting the nearby hills. Once in their shade, she slowed her stroll to an amble, roaming where fancy took her, and stopping to peer at anything which caught her fancy as she went. It was a pity that her thoughts, unbidden, kept returning to her stay in Alkmaar, and naturally enough, to Constantijn van Lindemann. She had really done her best to forget him, but without much success, which seemed strange when she realised that Archie Dukes had already faded into a pleasant nothing…a memory she didn't even bother to stir up, whereas Constantijn's image she was unable to throw out—and it wasn't as if the image was an altogether pleasing one. He had been downright rude; he had poked fun at her on several occasions—and he didn't like her hair. She picked up a lock and examined it in the sunbeams between the trees. He was right, of course, it was carroty. It was a pity that it didn't curl. She wandered on, pondering the possibility of tinting it—or going blonde.

While she had stopped to consider this knotty problem she became aware of a noise. It was faint; an animal or a child—she wasn't sure which. She kept very still trying to decide its direction, and when she heard it for the second time, she knew that it came from the old disused quarry on her left. She had just passed the battered sign warning anyone from going any nearer. The sound came again and this time she was certain that it was a child crying. The noise became even clearer as she approached the edge of the quarry, which should have been fenced off, but in parts wasn't. She was terrified of heights; Augusta swallowed carefully, took a breath, closed her eyes, then opened them again and looked over its edge. Below, a long way down, she saw shudderingly, was a child lying on the ground. There was a dog too—a labrador, or some similar breed, lying close and mounting guard. With an effort, Augusta tore her eyes from the depths below her and looked around seeking the least difficult way down. To her left there was a heap of smallish flints, piled against the side of the quarry, but not quite reaching its rim, but she thought she might be able to reach them. She worked round the edge until she stood directly above them, then lowered herself carefully over the edge; it took her minutes to scramble to the top of the heap, for her fright made her clumsy. When she did at last get there, she sat for a few seconds with her eyes closed before beginning to wriggle painfully down to the bottom.

The child was still crying. Augusta, tingling painfully from the flints, made her way over the rough boulders which strewed the floor of the quarry, and knelt down beside him. The dog whined, but didn't move. She said 'Good dog' automatically and turned her attention to the child. He was small—four or five perhaps; his arm hung awkwardly beside him and he had several cuts on his face and head. He was pale too—probably slightly concussed, although he was conscious for the moment at least. She said cheerfully:

'Hullo, love. Have you been here a long time?' He gulped a yes. 'And you fell?' He muttered yes again.

'What luck you had your dog with you. What's his name?'

'Rex.'

Augusta thought she recognised him then. 'Buller's Farm?' she hazarded, and was rewarded by a nod. It was in a way bad news, for the Bullers had six small children who roamed the countryside at will—probably Mrs Buller wouldn't notice that this particular offspring was missing until teatime. She would have to do something about his arm too. It looked like a fractured clavicle, which wasn't too bad provided there was nothing else broken. She began to feel his arms and legs very gently; they seemed whole—he even consented to move his legs and his one sound arm; if she could make a sling... She thought, rather wildly, that a white cotton petticoat would have been just the thing—she could have torn it into strips, like the heroines in TV Westerns. Instead, she took off her blouse and after a good deal of wrenching and tugging, tore a strip off the bottom. This made the blouse so short that it really wasn't decent any more; not that it mattered, for there was no one to see, although, as things stood, she wouldn't have minded if there had been.

She held the small arm firmly and turned the boy over the better to get at it, and he cried a great deal while she rolled her hanky into a ball and pushed it into his armpit, then carefully eased the arm across his bony chest and fastened the rather unsatisfactory sling. The dog made things difficult too, under the impression that she was up to some mischief; she could hardly blame the beast for tearing the seat of

her pants in the mistaken belief that he was helping
his small companion. It didn't matter anyway, her
slacks had been ruined by the flints on the way down.
She laid the boy flat again, in case he had concussion,
and searched around until she found a tuft of coarse
grass which she dragged from the unyielding ground
and put under his head. She would have liked water
to bathe his cuts, but this was out of the question. She
eyed the dog, wondering if he could be persuaded to
go home—someone seeing him alone might possibly
come in search of the child—if they knew where he
was... But the dog refused to budge. He wasn't a
young dog anyway. She doubted if he would be able
to climb up the quarry without an encouraging companion, and that certainly not without the boy.

Which put her in mind of her own plight. The child
was small but still too heavy for her even if she could
carry him up the impossible side, besides she would
hurt his arm dreadfully. She told him in a cheerful
voice that she was going to look for a way up, and
set out to explore, but it was a waste of time. She
didn't think she could get herself out, let alone carry
a child and urge a dog as well. They would have to
wait until someone came by. She told the boy this,
aware that the chance of someone passing was so remote as to be laughable. Only she didn't feel like
laughing because she was by now getting scared.

The child seemed easier after a little while, and
presently closed his eyes, although she wasn't sure if
he was asleep or unconscious. She would have to risk
disturbing him and try shouting. Her voice echoed
and re-echoed round the quarry, bringing no result
other than the disturbing of some indignant wood pi-
geons high above their heads. They had been sitting

almost an hour and she was getting desperate as well as hoarse, for she had been shouting at regular intervals. It was only a little after half past four and warm and airless in the quarry. She was sitting at the boy's head, screening him from the sun, and the dog, forgetful of his harsh treatment of her slacks, had wedged himself as close as possible to them both. She put an arm around his shoulders and asked to no purpose, but because it gave a little comfort, 'Oh, Rex, what are we going to do?'

The boy was still very quiet, though his pulse and colour were good, probably he was exhausted with fright and was sleeping it off...and a good thing too, it would be bad enough when he wakened. Augusta took a deep breath and shouted once more, and when a voice called 'Hullo there!' she didn't believe it. All the same, she tried again, adding hopefully, 'In the quarry,' in a voice which cracked with excitement and relief.

She was totally unprepared for Constantijn's appearance above her. He stood nonchalantly on the very edge, looking down at them. She was too far away to see his expression, but she had no doubt that it was amused, for she seemed to amuse him a good deal, and now surely more than ever.

He asked, 'What in the name of heaven are you doing down there?' his voice casual and, as she had known, faintly amused. Her almost hysterical relief at seeing him was swallowed in rage. She called back with quivering asperity, 'Having a picnic, of course...' and then, in case he were to believe it, 'Don't go—please don't go. The boy's hurt, and I don't know how to get us out. I'm not very good at climbing.'

She heard his rumbling laugh as he came down to her, moving fast and with an apparent carelessness which kept her heart in her mouth. But her fears for him were groundless—he fetched up beside her, a little dusty about the shoes, but otherwise unruffled. His unhurried voice had an edge to it, though. 'I had no intention of going away, though I doubt if you'll believe that. What happened?'

It was annoying that her own voice sounded so small and scared.

'Oh, no—I—I heard you laughing.'

He was already on his knees by the child, but he looked up as she spoke.

'I laughed because we meet again in this most unlikely of spots.'

He turned his attention to the child again and spoke without looking at her. 'Stop being so scared and tell me about the child.'

She told him, and when she had finished, he said, 'You did very well. He's probably concussed, but not badly, I think, and beyond that clavicle I can't feel any broken bones, but we must get him to hospital. I'll go first—I think if I sling him over my shoulder so'—he suited the action to the words—'that gives me a free hand for the dog, though I fancy he'll manage. You follow behind me—it's not as bad as it looks.'

He gave her a sharp glance as he spoke and asked, 'How did you get down?'

'I slid down that heap of flints.' She stood silent, frowning, expecting him to laugh. He didn't even smile, nor did he speak, only stared until he said merely, 'Come on.' and that abruptly as he turned his back and began to make his way to the selfsame heap.

It was all right to begin with—she fixed her eyes resolutely upon his feet, planting hers as nearly as possible in the same places. She was sick with fright, but now was hardly the time to tell him that she had a terror of heights. They were perhaps a third of the way up when by some perverse chance, she looked down. The floor of the quarry seemed miles below her; it swam and see-sawed and its steep sides melted and slid around her so that she was no longer sure if her feet were planted firmly or not. She closed her eyes, then opened them again and tried to drag them away from the heaving ground just as the stone she was clinging to slipped from her hand. She watched it roll faster and faster, down to the bottom, while she sought frantically for something solid to cling to once more. She wanted desperately to scream, even to utter a cry for help, but she decided against it; the doctor couldn't stop now—not with the child slung across his shoulders and the dog to urge on; besides, he would be almost at the top.

She watched in helpless fascination while the walls of the quarry swayed and dipped around her, and wondered if she would be able to hold on. She would have to. She longed to see how far he had got, but she didn't dare to move, indeed, she could not, locked as she was in an icy panic which suddenly got the better of her, so that she opened her mouth to scream and then bit the sound off as he called calmly:

'Lean against the flints, Augusta—press into them. And relax, dear girl, relax, you aren't going to fall. I'm coming down.'

His voice quietened her, so that she did as she was told with a slow clumsiness. It seemed an age before she heard him coming and felt his arm around her shoulders. She relaxed completely then. She had never felt so safe, and when he said in the same unhurried calm voice:

'You're going to hold my hand, and we shall climb up to the top together, Augusta,' she managed to turn her head to look at him.

'I can't,' she said flatly, 'I feel sick.'

His smile became tinged with gentle mockery. 'Good lord, girl, take a hold of yourself. Here's my hand. You shall be as sick as you like once we're at the top.'

She answered childishly, 'I'm so frightened...' then stopped because she wasn't really frightened any more, at least, only a very little. His smile lost its mockery, leaving a tenderness which made her close her eyes. When she opened them a second later, he wasn't smiling at all. She swallowed carefully. 'No, I'm not frightened any more now. You're not, are you?'

His eyebrows soared. 'No, but then I'm not allergic to heights and you obviously are, Augusta. Did you slide down with your eyes shut?' She nodded. 'You must be sore.'

She nodded again. 'Rex tore my slacks too.'

'Yes, I noticed. You're barely decent.'

She gave the ghost of a giggle and in that moment found herself inexplicably on her feet, her hand in his cool firm grasp.

It was surprising how easy it was, after all. Just the same, when they stood at last on the rough grass, with the little boy and the dog lying close by, she turned a white face to his and said with hurried and wholly unnecessary politeness, 'Excuse me...' and fled, only to find him beside her when it was over, mopping her up very efficiently with a large white handkerchief. Presently, almost herself again, she said:

'Thank you, that was kind. I'm all right now. I'm sorry I funked...'

He interrupted her quite sharply. 'Nonsense. If you had—er—funked it, you wouldn't have gone down in the first place.' He pulled her to her feet. 'Let's get this child to hospital.'

He picked the little boy up and started off through the coarse grass and the dense thicket, the dog and Augusta hard on his heels.

'Are you sure this child's from Buller's?' he asked over his shoulder as they went.

'Yes—they're on the telephone. Perhaps they will let us ring up from the hospital.'

He grunted, 'Good idea,' and they went on in silence until they reached the wider, rougher track she had followed earlier in the afternoon. They walked side by side, the dog padding along between them. Constantijn spared her a brief glance. 'All right? The car's not far.'

She didn't reply, only nodded, for she was tired and hot and sore in a great many places, and over and above all this, she was extremely happy.

The Rolls stood by the side of the narrow road, sleek and polished and exuding a quiet power which didn't need advertisement. Like its owner, thought Augusta, as he helped her in, put the child carefully on her lap, ushered Rex into the back of the car and got in himself. They drove in silence while she pondered the fact that he should be there at all. After her first surprise, his appearance had seemed quite natural at the quarry, but that was because she had been scared and had wanted him. She was prevented from following this interesting train of thought by the child on her lap, whose sudden restlessness held her attention until they reached the hospital at Sherborne. It should have surprised her that the doctor seemed well known there, but somehow it seemed perfectly natural. The boy was whisked away, Constantijn went off to telephone Buller's Farm and she herself was led away to a cubicle where she was given what he had called 'the appropriate and soothing treatment', and joined him again in time to hear that Mr Buller was already on his way to the hospital and that the X-rays confirmed a mild concussion and the fractured clavicle.

'You don't mind if we wait until the boy's father gets here?' Constantijn wanted to know. Augusta shook her head and accepted a cup of tea, but Mr Buller arrived before she had time to finish it. She listened while the doctor explained what had happened. He told the story succinctly, with due emphasis on her prompt and level-headed behaviour, so that she blushed hotly, hideously aware of tangled hair and torn clothes. She endured Mr Buller's thanks politely, promised to telephone him later to find out about the little boy, and went outside to the car with Constantijn, who, having restored Rex to his master, held the door open for her. But she held back. 'It was very kind of you to rescue us,' she began inadequately. 'I won't keep you any longer—I hope we haven't spoilt your afternoon. I'll—I'll telephone someone to come for me.'

He didn't appear to have heard a word she had been saying, but, 'Do get in,' he said in a mild no-nonsense voice, so that she did so. Only after he had turned into the main road did she venture to remark that he would need to take a turning.

'Yes, I know. Niptree Petherton, the stone house standing back from the road on the left, just before you come to the church. Funny, I must have passed it a hundred times.'

She echoed faintly, 'A hundred times?' and shot him a startled glance. 'You don't live here as well as in Alkmaar?'

He laughed. 'Well, no, but Dr Soames is my godfather. When he needs a holiday or feels off colour I get my partner to look after my side of the practice and come over. It's strange that we've never met before.'

Augusta let this pass. 'I didn't know Dr Soames was ill.'

He negotiated a corner before he answered. 'He's not. I wrote and asked him if he knew of a vet by the name of Brown who lived on the Somerset-Dorset border and owned a donkey called Bottom.'

Augusta digested this in silence. She thought of several answers and discarded them all. She said instead, 'We keep meeting.'

'So we do,' he agreed silkily. 'Do you mind?'

'No.' She took a quick look at his profile—the arrogant nose and the high forehead, the firm curved mouth with the familiar little smile at its corners. She knew then what had happened to her and why she had felt so happy. She was in love with him. The idea made her feel peculiar and set her pulse racing, but her happiness oozed slowly away before the doubt that he felt the same about her. She blinked her beautiful eyes against the sudden warmth of tears and when he remarked mildly, 'I thought I'd come over for a few days,' she was able to reply in a cheerful voice that it was a nice time of year to have a break and the country looked wonderful. It was fortunate that he was turning the car between the gateposts of her home, for she could think of nothing further to say except a rather breathless goodbye. But he got out too and went round the car's bonnet to help her out and walked to the door with her. 'Your mother asked me to come back,' he explained casually.

Augusta paused in the open doorway. 'Mother? When did you see Mother?'

'This afternoon,' he explained patiently. 'I called to see you and your mother told me where you might be and asked me back for tea.' He looked at his watch. 'We're a bit late, I'm afraid.'

She led the way to the back of the house and opened the kitchen door. Her mother was at the table in the centre of the old-fashioned, comfortable kitchen, carefully turning a cake out of its tin. She looked up as they went in.

'There you are—how late.' Consternation swept over her face. 'Roly, whatever has happened?'

Augusta turned in time to see a quiver, instantly suppressed, pass over the doctor's face, and went pink. The pink deepened when her mother came nearer, to take in her tattered appearance in one all-embracing glance. 'Your blouse—and you've grazed your arm—and your slacks! Darling, they're in ribbons! Why, I can see your b—'

'Mother!' said Augusta awfully, and fled upstairs.

She came down ten minutes later, to find the doctor leaning against the kitchen dresser, his hands in his pockets, on the best of terms with her mother. They both looked up as she went in; her mother's look was quick and missed nothing, the doctor's was leisurely and it also missed nothing. She had washed her face and hands and tugged the tangles out of her hair, and with the perversity of the female in love, had chosen to put on a mouse-coloured linen dress which rendered her as inconspicuous as her hair and eyes would allow. Her mother turned away at once and said briskly, 'I've made the tea, darling—you must be dying for a cup, and I've cut the cake. Constantijn doesn't mind the kitchen.'

Augusta advanced to the table and sat down on the chair he had thoughtfully pulled out for her. Constantijn indeed, she thought with a sudden flash of temper—he had, of course, turned on the charm. Obedient to her mother's request, she put milk in three cups, refusing to look at him, nor did she look up when her mother sat down opposite her, indicating that their guest should sit beside her.'

'How beastly for you, darling, stuck in the old quarry like that. Going down must have been awful, all on your own. Did you shut your eyes?' Augusta nodded, drinking tea. 'Constantijn tells me you were sick afterwards,' went on her mother, with all the loving tactlessness of a doting parent. 'Do you remember the time the Grant boys dared you to go up the church tower? You were bilious for days after.'

Augusta, who loved her mother dearly, threw her a waspish look. 'I was ten, Mother,' she explained painstakingly. She caught Constantijn's look and was instantly aware that he was trying to imagine what she looked like at that age. She offered him more cake to distract his thought, but without success, for he asked blandly, Why are you called Roly?'

She looked at her mother, who had pretended not

to hear. 'It's a silly name that Charles—my brother—
used to call me when I was a little girl.' She paused.
'I was fat.' She gave him a defiant look, which he
countered with a stare as bland as his voice had been.

'I find that hard to believe,' and then, to infuriate
her, 'You seem to have—er—trimmed it down very
nicely.'

Augusta spoke with dignity. 'I've never done a
thing about it, it just went, and it's never come back,
I stay the same,' and went brightly pink when he murmured, 'And a very delightful same, too,' forestalling
any answer she might have made by glancing at his
watch with the remark that he would be forced to go
as he had promised to take his godfather's evening
surgery. He got up and Mrs Brown said comfortably,
'Well, do come again—any time you've half an hour
to spare, you might like to see round the dispensary.'

Augusta went with him to the door, wondering
when she would see him again. It was a pity that she
would have to go back to hospital in three days' time,
and tomorrow was the Jumble Sale and she had promised to go with her mother. He stopped by the front
door, standing beside her, saying nothing. For lack of
anything better, she asked, 'How can you take Dr
Soames' surgery?—I mean, you're a foreigner.'

He smiled a little. 'I've a Cambridge degree as well
as Leiden.' She waited for him to enlarge a little upon
this; apparently he didn't intend to, so to fill another
awkward gap, she said, 'Oh, I see—it must make
havoc of your own practice.' He made no comment
upon this either and she was forced to be satisfied
with this morsel of information about him. She tried
to picture him at Cambridge and wondered how old
he was; she should have asked the aunts. The silence

having got a little out of hand, she said politely, 'Thank you for helping us out of the quarry.'

'It was a pleasure,' he said on a laugh. 'I don't know when I have enjoyed myself so much'; and with the touchiness of the newly in love she snapped, 'Well, I'm glad you found it amusing!'

He raised his brows. 'Did I say that I was amused?' he queried softly. He turned to go and she longed to be able to say something so interesting and compelling that he would stay, even if only for a few minutes. Instead she mumbled goodbye and watched him get into his car and drive away.

When she got back to the kitchen her mother was pottering to and fro, getting supper. Augusta went over to the sink and started to wash the tea things with her back safely towards her mother's eye. Presently she said brightly, 'Constantijn liked your cake, darling—it was super.'

Her mother said 'Yes, dear,' in a thoughtful voice and Augusta braced herself for the steady flow of questions she expected. But they weren't forthcoming. Beyond observing that she had fancied the doctor to be a much older and duller man. Mrs Brown said nothing, which was far worse than the questions would have been, for Augusta was longing to talk about him.

The Jumble Sale was to be opened at three o'clock, but the committee ladies were at the Vicarage, where it was to be held, long before that hour. Augusta, who had taken her mother down in the car, made herself generally useful, setting out tea-cups and filling kettles in the huge Victorian kitchen at the other end of the house. This done, she helped to arrange the vast mass of things for sale on the various tables and

benches set out in the drawing room. She rather enjoyed this—it was fun to recognise the various hats
that had been in church each Sunday morning
throughout the winter, and drape dresses and coats
with all the wrong hemlines. The shoes too—evening
slippers, as good as new and hopelessly out of date;
discarded wellington boots, and last summer's sandals. She helped with the White Elephant stall too and
noted several odds and ends of china worth buying.

There was a fairing there, a married couple, sitting
sedately side by side in bed with the words 'Married
Bliss' painted in gold letters on the bedhead, and a
tiny Victorian pincushion in velvet, heart-shaped and
beautifully embroidered in beadwork. She wanted that
too; she was contemplating doing a secret deal with
the curate's wife, who was in charge of the stall, when
Mrs Grimble, the vicar's wife, bore down upon her.
'There's such a crowd outside,' she announced happily. 'Augusta, will you go and put another kettle
on—there's a large one in the stillroom. We never
use it, but we will today.' She beamed with great
good humour at Augusta, whom she had known since
she was a baby, and went away to meet the first rush
of visitors as the garden gate was opened.

Augusta trailed off again through the house, which
was large, rambling and badly planned. She reached
the kitchen and went through it, pausing to inspect
her person in the long mirror which some bygone
owner had hung on the wall of the small, unnamed
room leading out of it. She had always liked to think
that the maids were able to make use of it when they
weren't toiling up and down the numerous staircases.
She poked at a few hairpins to make sure that they
were secure, examined a bruise on one arm, and

smoothed her dress. It was of lawn, with a full skirt and a great many small tucks on the bodice, it had long ballooning sleeves with tight cuffs, and its colour was a very pale, soft yellow. She hadn't worn it before and the only reason she had put it on now was because she wanted to look her best just in case she should meet Constantijn. That the village jumble sale was the last place he was likely to visit made it all the more important that she should look nice.

She sighed deeply, squinted horribly at her reflection, and went in search of the kettle. It proved hard to find, for the stillroom door was locked, which meant that she had to search through the kitchen until she found the key—which she eventually did, in a jar marked Sugar in one of the many cupboards. She had been aware of faint clapping while she hunted; the opener, whoever he was, was obviously performing his task; she would never get back in time to buy the fairing or the pincushion. She poked around the stillroom and found the kettle—a huge castiron vessel from another age—and bore it gingerly back to the kitchen. She was halfway across its vast flagstoned floor when Constantijn came in from the opposite door.

'Mrs Grimble said the kitchen,' he remarked casually, 'but she didn't warn me that it was a day's march away.' He took the kettle from her hand and examined it with some interest. 'Good God, what's this? A museum piece?' and when she didn't answer he gave her a cool stare and said, 'Augusta, close your mouth—you look exactly like a goldfish.'

She gave him a look of outrage. She had, after all, gone to a lot of trouble to dress with extra care, for although she hadn't expected to meet him, she had wanted to look her best if she did. She said rather crossly, 'That museum piece, as you call it, has to be cleaned and filled with water and put on the stove.'

'Well,' he said genially, 'you can't do it, not all dressed up like that.'

She allowed this unfeeling remark to pass without comment—she would deal with it later. Ignoring the amused lift of his eyebrows, she said merely, 'Thank you, Doctor. The sink's here.'

She led the way through another door into a small dark room, rather mousy and damp; it had an enormous stone sink in one corner with an innocuous heater above it. She watched while he cleaned the kettle, filled it with water and set it among its more modern fellows on a small enamel gas stove in the kitchen, where it was wedged between a bread oven and a blackleaded monstrosity which might have found favour with Mrs Beeton. This done, he went back to the sink to wash his hands.

'How are the sore places?' he wanted to know.

'I'm perfectly recovered, thank you.'

He had come to stand close beside her. 'You certainly look quite different—who do you intend to dazzle?'

Augusta adjusted a gas ring unnecessarily and without looking at him, said haughtily, 'I've no intention of dazzling anyone.' She would have liked to walk casually out of the kitchen and lose herself in the crowd, but he was looming over her in a way which made it difficult to pass him. She fixed her eyes on his waistcoat and waited. When he spoke his voice was silky. 'A pity. I hoped you might want to dazzle me.' He shrugged his broad shoulders. 'Are you chained to these kettles, or are you free to examine the delights of Mrs Grimble's drawing room?'

'Oh, I'm not a helper,' she explained, 'just odd jobs and things.'

'Good,' he caught her by the arm. 'I refuse to buy a cast-off hat, but there might be something on the White Elephant stall.'

'Oh, yes, there is,' agreed Augusta, very conscious of his hand on her arm, 'but they'll be gone…a fairing—a china figure,' she explained kindly because he was a foreigner and might not know. 'People used to buy them at fairs—and a velvet pincushion trimmed with beads. Someone will have snapped them up, though.' She sighed. 'I'll have to buy something, though—knitted dishcloths, I suppose, there are always dozens left over.' She brightened. 'But there are the raffles too.'

They had been walking without haste through the house. Now he opened the drawing room door. 'I can't wait!' he said. 'Take me to the dishcloths first, but there's someone you must meet on the way.'

It was the Brigadier. He was sitting in a large chair in a corner of the crowded room with his footless leg resting on a low stool; its trouser leg had been neatly pinned just above the ankle and he looked thin, but the smile he gave Augusta was positively gay. 'My dear gal,' he exclaimed, wringing her hand, 'Constantijn said he would find you—I'm staying with Doctor Soames for a night or so; promised to open this affair months ago; couldn't let them down.' He gave her hand a squeeze and let it go. 'Come and talk to me some time, but don't let me keep you from a look round first.'

She was led away to the dishcloths and when they

were out of earshot she said, 'He looks marvellous, I'm so glad.'

'I knew you would be—now tell me what to buy.'

She began to enjoy herself. Even though she was in love with him he frequently annoyed her, but today he was intent on being the perfect companion, just as he had been in Amsterdam. They wandered from one trestle table to another, buying jam and pickles, some old volumes of *Punch*, a flower vase with a chip in it and several packets of needles, because Augusta declared that they always came in useful. Of the fairing and the pincushion there was no trace—the White Elephant was swept all but clean, but there were still the raffles and the Hidden Treasure to discover for five pence a time. They were having a second chance at the bottle stall when she said regretfully, 'I must go. I promised to make the tea.'

Augusta wanted to tell him that she wouldn't be long, or ask him to wait for her, but probably he was waiting for a chance to go home. She smiled too brightly, added a bottle of sauce to the collection of things he was carrying, and made for the kitchen. It didn't take long to make the tea; in ten minutes the last of the volunteer waitresses had borne off their trays, leaving her to fill the kettles again with an eye to second cups—there was always a brisk trade with cups of tea at village functions. She tidied up neatly and went back to the drawing room, where she was pounced upon immediately by Constantijn carrying two cups of tea. He said briefly, 'Over here,' and led the way to an abandoned table, flicked its corner with his handkerchief and said, 'Jump up,' then handed her her tea. 'How long does this—er—function last?'

Augusta drank her tea. 'Another half hour or so.'

Her eyes swept the room. 'They look as though they've almost sold out, but you can go when you like, you know. You've been very generous.'

His cheerful agreement rather disconcerted her. 'But,' he added, 'as this is the first and probably the last time I shall ever attend such an occasion I don't grudge a penny of it. Have you finished your odd jobs?'

She remembered the kettles and hesitated, but before she could speak he went on, 'Ah, yes, the kettles, I think we should deal with them.'

Augusta eyed him doubtfully. He looked friendly and kind, smiling at her like that. She wished she knew him well enough to be certain that he wasn't just being polite. 'Well, yes—what I mean is—you don't need to bother, you've been very kind already.'

'You've just said something like that,' he observed blandly. 'What endears me to you, Augusta Brown, is your desire to be rid of my company, and your firm resolution to carry it out.'

She blushed and rushed into unguarded speech. 'Oh, no, I don't want you to go at all. I thought you might be finding it all a bit dull—that is—it's not very exciting for you.'

'Do I look the kind of man who needs to be excited? No, don't answer that. You will just have to believe me when I tell you that I have been excited all the afternoon.' He smiled at her in such a manner that she was forced to gulp her heart back into its proper place. 'By you, my dear Augusta,' he finished.

Her heart, quite out of control, thumped against her ribs, finally she managed to say, 'I'm glad you enjoyed it.' Which remark he received with a short laugh of genuine amusement as he took her arm and

walked her back to the kitchen once more, where he
dealt with the kettles, and then, with the air of a man
goaded beyond his normal powers of endurance,
caught her firmly round her slim waist and kissed her,
not once, but several times with a deliberate enjoy-
ment.

Augusta went back to St Jude's the next morning,
explaining to her astonished parents that she had quite
forgotten a lecture she had promised to attend. That
it was Sunday had escaped her muddled mind, and
they, realising that something had gone awry for their
Roly, weren't going to make matters worse by re-
minding her. She had gone down to breakfast with a
pale unhappy face, looking as though she hadn't
closed her eyes during the entire night, which indeed
was true, save for a brief heavy sleep as the early
dawn broke. Her mother longed to ask her what was
wrong, but she knew her Augusta too well for that.
She was, after all, a sensible girl and twenty-three.
They drove her into Sherborne to catch a late morning
train and as it pulled out of the station, her mother
called:

'I'll write, darling,' which Augusta rightly understood to mean, 'I'll write and tell you when Constantijn has gone.'

She stared woodenly out of the window for the
whole journey, while convincing herself that she
wasn't running away, but retreating from a situation
which was rapidly becoming impossible. He had said
in Alkmaar that there was no harm in their meeting.
She recalled how lightly he had said it, because for
him it was doubtless a light matter, but it was no such
thing for her. The thought of never seeing him again

was almost not to be endured, but equally, meeting him again would be far worse. She resolutely forced her thoughts away from him and wondered about Susan Belsize instead. But this, in its way, was just as bad. Watching the dreary, smoke-grimed backs of London's houses as they blotted out the countryside, she reflected on the strange coincidence that Dr Soames should be Constantijn's godfather—but then it had been coincidence that he should have a practice in Alkmaar. She closed her eyes against the depressing backyards and strings of washing, and fell into a brief doze which lasted until she was jerked awake at Paddington Station.

She left her case in her room at the hospital and filled the rest of the wasted day with a bus ride to Richmond Park, where she walked until she was too tired to think any more, and on her return, she countered her friends' astonished comments on her early return by inventing some absolutely vital shopping which she needed to do on Monday morning. Having invented an excuse, it was necessary to live up to it. She went out early and bought, rather defiantly, a Terlenka trouser suit, white with a tunic top; it made her green eyes greener than ever, and gave her carroty hair a burnish.

The next day, going off duty, she went, idly enough for she didn't expect any post, to look for letters. There was a small package for her; it contained two carefully tissue paper wrapped boxes with a brief note from her mother: 'Roly darling, Constantijn brought these round and asked me to see that you got them.'

She unwrapped them carefully. One contained the fairing from the White Elephant stall, the other held the little velvet pincushion.

was almost not to be endured, but equally meeting
him again would be far worse. She resolutely forced
her thoughts away from him and wondered about Sir
Ian before he... she forced her mind away, had me
and Watching the cheery, smoke-grimed faces of

CHAPTER SIX

TWO DAYS LATER Augusta received an invitation from
Lady Belway, this time for luncheon. The note, written with an old-fashioned nib and heavily underlined,
was couched in terms to touch all but the most hard-
hearted, and Augusta was soft-hearted. Nurse, it
seemed, was on holiday; the writer was alone, ready
to die of a combination of ennui and bad temper.

Augusta, in her dressing gown after a long day's
work, penned her acceptance in a neat handwriting,
while her closer friends, with the inevitable mugs of
tea, bore her company. She addressed the envelope,
oblivious of the buzz of talk around her and the shrill
whine of some pop group belting out their latest effort
from her radio. She stuck out her tongue and licked
the envelope flap as Mary Wilkes leaned across the
bed. 'Finished?' she inquired in a subdued shout. 'I'll
post it for you as I go past the warden's lodge—here's
your tea. What will you wear?' The absorbing topic
engaged their full attention for the best part of five
minutes, then: 'Guess who I saw today, outside the
Coq d'Or in Stratton Street.'

'Whatever were you doing in Stratton Street?' inquired Augusta.

'Oh, I can't remember. It was that gorgeous girl
who used to visit your old Lady Belway—in a lime
green dress, ducky, very eye-catching. She had that
fair-haired giant with her—the one who was always
with her here in PP, and was his eye caught!' She

made an expressive grimace and Augusta heard her own voice answering quite normally, although she didn't feel in the least normal. 'She wears the most super clothes. I wonder where she gets them?'

Augusta didn't want to know in the least, but it was as good a red herring as any. It really was most unfair, for she had been trying hard not to think of Constantijn and for the last few days she had managed rather well although she had cheated a little, because the first things she saw when she awoke each morning were the fairing and the pincushion side by side on her bed-table. It was foolish to leave them there, where they could remind her; she had hidden them away one evening, determined not to look at them again, and had then had to get out of bed in the middle of the night because she couldn't sleep for thinking of them buried deep under a pile of undies.

Mary said carelessly, 'Oh, one of those wildly expensive shops with a bowl of flowers and a scarf in the window, I shouldn't wonder. Did you ever get to know him? He looks rather nice.'

Augusta was not to be drawn. 'Nice enough,' she replied airily, 'not quite our world, though. How's Archie these days?'

Mary's nice face puckered. 'You wouldn't like him back again, I suppose?' she asked. 'There's a marvellous new CO—he hasn't asked me out yet, but I think he might, only Archie...'

Augusta nodded. She and Mary were good friends. Archie was sweet but was not, so to speak, a permanent proposition. She asked now, 'I say, is Archie getting serious about you?'

Mary looked amazed. 'Lord, no. He just likes to take a girl to the flicks—you know.'

Augusta nodded again. 'Then you'll have to find someone else for him to go out with,' she suggested practically. 'That'll leave you free to dally with the CO'

Mary eyed her thoughtfully. 'Anyone in mind?' she asked. They looked around them until their eyes lighted upon a small creature, her mug clasped in her hands while she listened to her companions arguing hotly as to whose turn it was to have the bathroom first. They stared at her and then looked at each other. 'She's just right for Archie,' said Mary, 'and we'd be doing her a good turn. We'll get to work on them both.'

They shook hands solemnly and Mary went on, 'Good, that's settled. What's the matter, Gussie?— you're different. Ever since you came back from holiday. You didn't mind about Archie?'

'Heavens, no.' Augusta spoke with sincerity. 'I think perhaps I want a change—you know, the same old grind—which reminds me...'

She finished her tea, switched off the radio and advised her companions that as she had an Early the next morning, she had better get some sleep. But sleep didn't come, instead she lay very wide awake wondering about Constantijn and Susan. For it must be because of Susan that he was in England. It was pure chance that he had heard that she lived in the same village as Dr Soames; he had just happened to be there and anything he had said was in order to make himself agreeable, although this last idea didn't really hold water, for he had at times been very disagreeable and she didn't think he was the sort of man to put himself out. It seemed a good idea to stop thinking about him and concentrate on the luncheon party instead. This she did to be instantly brought up short by the thought that he might possibly be going too. Well, she couldn't back out now—Sister had given her a day off and she couldn't possibly ask her to change it again. She drifted off into a fitful sleep, still worrying about it.

She was a little pale with excitement when she rang the bell at Lady Belway's front door. She had put on the white dress with the black patent slingbacks and the matching handbag, and as it was a glorious day she hadn't bothered with a coat. If it chose to rain on the way back, she would just have to take a taxi. Her heart beat a little faster as she followed the butler up the stairs, not wanting to see Constantijn again but thinking how wonderful it would be if he were there. He wasn't, but the Brig, was, sitting spruce and erect beside Lady Belway's day bed.

He greeted her with as much pleasure as her hostess, and over their sherry wanted to know why she hadn't gone back to talk to him at the Jumble Sale. To her annoyance she went red, but before she could say anything, he remarked, 'I'm teasing you, and that's unfair, isn't it? Constantijn didn't give you a chance, did he? Pity you had to come back to hospital so unexpectedly, though—he spent the whole morning tracking a pincushion of all things and one of those china fairings—said you wanted them. Did you get them?' He turned a blue gimlet eye upon her and Augusta said 'Yes, thank you,' in a faint voice, and was saved from uttering anything else by Providence in the shape of the butler announcing lunch.

Getting the two old people to the dining room needed the help of herself and two young maids who had obviously done it all before, for they took no notice, in a respectful way, of their mistress's commands and counter commands, but walked her stolidly between them. Augusta found herself with the Brigadier, who managed very well with her shoulder and a crutch. They were almost at the dining room door when he stopped and asked gruffly, 'Well, what do you think of young Constantijn, eh?'

She had been taken by surprise, but she said carefully, 'He—he seems very nice, I think. He was most helpful getting us out of that quarry.' She cast around in her head for something else noncommittal. 'He was most generous at the Jumble Sale,' she added a little uncertainly.

The Brig became suddenly peppery—indeed, she formed the opinion that if he had had a foot to stamp, he would have stamped it. As it was he exclaimed explosively, 'God bless my soul, gal, I asked you a plain question and you give me some bread and butter answer about Constantijn being nice! If you don't want to give me your honest opinion, don't.'

She said instantly, 'Good, I won't,' and he gave a brief laugh, not in the least put out. He sat down to table in high good humour and didn't mention Constantijn again, but led the conversation round to cricket and then, followed a little guardedly by Augusta, to Holland. But she need not have worried; her companions reminisced gently, recounting delightful tales of their own travels in their youth and inviting her to add to them. They lunched at length, starting with cold cucumber soup and going on to *Filets de Sole Véronique*, followed by pheasant and a champagne icecream, Augusta had never heard of, much less eaten. It was served in tall glasses with a spiral of lemon peel on top, and she thought that she had never tasted anything so marvellous, and the champagne, combining nicely with the wine she had already had, had the pleasant effect of making life seem brighter than it had been of late.

They went back to the drawing room for coffee, and soon afterwards she got up to go despite Lady Belway's plea that she should stay for another hour or so, but the Brigadier had made no move when she did and she guessed that they would probably have a good gossip when she had gone; besides, she hardly counted herself as one of Lady Belway's friends. But although she won her point on going back to the hospital, she couldn't avoid her hostess's insistence that she should be driven back to St Jude's. She made her farewells and followed the butler downstairs and out of the front door, to find an old-fashioned Daimler, most beautifully maintained, waiting for her. The chauffeur was almost as old as the butler and just as benevolent in his manner. She was about to step into this equipage, attended assiduously by these members of Lady Belway's household, when a small sports car, apparently appearing from nowhere, drew up behind the Daimler. Constantijn was at the wheel, Susan Belsize was beside him, looking, if that were possible, more beautiful than ever. She waved airily at Augusta, who, her healthy pink cheeks gone a little pale, waved back. Constantijn did nothing at all, merely stared at her with a pale penetrating look which could so disconcert her. She smiled at him uncertainly because he looked so forbidding, and got into the Daimler and was borne smoothly away, stifling a great desire to turn round and have a look at him as she went.

She had promised to go out with Mary and Archie and the new CO that evening; not because she partic-

ularly wanted to, but to do Mary a good turn. Now
she wished she had never said that she would go; it
was going to be difficult to concentrate on Archie
when all the time her thoughts would be of Constantijn, and heaven knows they were muddled enough,
tearing around inside her head like squirrels in a cage.
It was a relief when one of her friends banged on her
bedroom door and begged her to make up a foursome
for tennis until teatime. It was when the four of them
were strolling off the tennis court, rather hot and
breathless, that the wooden gate leading to the path
across the Nurses' Home grounds, was flung open and
Constantijn, very much at ease, strolled towards them.
He exchanged greetings with charming politeness,
took Augusta firmly by the arm, and with some easy
excuse which she was too surprised to hear, walked
her rapidly away. When they were a little distance
from the others he stopped, and still with a hand on
her arm, turned her round to face him. 'You know,'
he said mildly, 'I came prepared to deal quite severely
with you, but now, seeing you like this with that carroty hair all over the place and that ridiculous short
skirt, I find I can't—it would be like bawling out Johanna.'

Augusta fidgeted uneasily, not looking at him, and
then overcome by curiosity, asked, 'Why should you
want to bawl me out?'

He said, quite ill-tempered, 'What's all this about
some fairytale lecture? Whoever heard of any self-
respecting honorary lecturing on a Sunday?' She
didn't answer at once and he gave her a little shake—
a gentle one. 'Well, was there a lecture?'

She steeled herself to meet his eye. 'No—and if

you want to know why I came back I'll tell you now it's none of your business.'

His voice was silky. 'My dear girl, don't anticipate me—why should I try to find out what I already know?'

She reddened under his gaze, angry and bewildered and caught off her guard. She snapped, 'Have you come to bait me? and how did you get in anyway?'

'Oh, I've influence,' he explained airily. His face suddenly became kind, just as it had been in the quarry. 'My dear Augusta Brown—' He smiled at her with tenderness so that her heart, which was already behaving in a most irregular fashion, stopped altogether and then began its beating afresh with a sudden fierce rush to shake her.

'Have dinner with me this evening?'

She wanted to say yes. For a brief second she thought of the delight of being in his company for a few hours. She shook her head. 'I can't—I'm going out...' He interrupted, 'With Archie?'

She nodded reluctantly, tempted to tell him about it, but when she took a quick peep at his face and saw that he didn't look in the least disappointed at her answer, she said nothing at all but stood, with his hand still on her arm, while he said cheerfully, 'Then I won't keep you, Augusta.' His hand dropped from her arm and she felt all at once bereft and lonely. The others had gone on; they started to walk side by side towards the gate, Augusta mulling over several questions she longed to ask and at last choosing the one least likely to be misconstrued, inquired:

'Are you busy?' then wished she hadn't spoken, for it couldn't have sounded sillier. He stood still, his hands in his pockets, jangling the loose change in them in an irritating manner. He appeared to be considering her question. He said slowly, 'Busy?—busy working or having fun—you don't say. At the moment I'm having fun, dear girl, my godfather's practice isn't so demanding that I can't have a day off occasionally. And you? Are you busy? Smoothing brows and pillows and learning how to be a good Ward Sister when you get the chance?' He was laughing a little, but his words sounded sourly in her ears, for that would be her ultimate future—she couldn't visualise wanting to marry anyone but him. She had a lightning glimpse of herself in ten years' time, her carroty hair a little dull, and she herself a little dull too, running a ward with the efficiency of someone who had no other interest in life. Without her knowing it, the soft curves of her mouth turned down and Constantijn said, 'Don't look at ghosts that aren't there, Augusta Brown. Enjoy your evening.' Which left her nothing further to say except a muttered goodbye before she walked away rather fast in the direction of the Nurses' Home.

The evening for the other three was highly successful, though hardly for Augusta, who laughed and talked to hide a misery which actually hurt while she thought of all the things she could have said, and hadn't, to Constantijn. She was listening to Archie theorising about some peculiar case he had admitted that day when she remembered that she had never thanked Constantijn for the fairing and the pincushion, and the consternation upon her face showed itself so strongly that Archie stopped in the middle of a sentence and begged her not to take the patient's condition too much to heart.

Before she went to bed that night, she wrote a stiff

little note to Constantijn thanking him for his gifts and addressed it care of Dr Soames, for she had no idea where he was; probably back in Alkmaar by now, she decided as she composed herself for the sleep which eluded her for a great part of the night.

There was a bad multiple car crash in the following morning. The ward filled up at a moment's notice with patients whose injuries needed the constant care which did not allow of any other thoughts than those concerned with the job in hand. Augusta, who had stayed on duty to help with the rush, got to her room after nine o'clock, too tired to do more than bath, drink the tea Mary had made for her, and fall into bed to sleep dreamlessly until she was called the next morning. The days which followed were almost as bad, for there were nurses on holiday and a senior student nurse off sick. Augusta welcomed the hard work and extra time on duty, for there was no time to think on duty, and when she was free she was too weary to be bothered. But at the end of three or four days, the ward staff was full strength again, with patients improved or transferred to Intensive Care: she was able to drink her coffee with Sister in the mornings once more and go off duty on time.

She had an unexpected weekend off too, for Sister had asked her to change with her, and had offered her a half-day to add on to it to make up for the off duty she had missed. It meant that she would be able to go home on Thursday evening and stay until Tuesday morning as she wouldn't have to go on duty until after midday dinner. She had heard from her mother that Constantijn had gone and come back and was returning to Holland within a couple of days, so that she would be able to go home without fear of meeting him—a situation which her common sense told her was most satisfactory but which her heart deplored despite the fact that she had decided that she wouldn't willingly see him again. She waited a day, trying to decide whether to go home or not, and made up her mind finally to telephone her mother in the evening. But her mother telephoned first during tea, and Augusta, called to the telephone, asked anxiously through a mouthful of bread and butter, 'Mother, are you all right? Is something the matter?'

Her parent's voice, sounding very cheerful, hastened to reassure her. 'Roly, you can't possibly change your weekend, can you?' her mother wanted to know.

'That's funny,' said Augusta, 'I was going to phone you this evening. I'm free until Tuesday midday, starting tomorrow evening…I'm coming home.'

'No, darling,' said her mother briskly, 'you're not. You're coming over to Alkmaar with me—it's all arranged. The aunts want to see me and it's such a good opportunity, and I said if you could get off you would come too.'

Augusta became aware of a peculiar sensation, rather like being in a dream; an interested spectator who was powerless to alter the sequence of the events taking place. She asked, a little breathless, 'Mother, what have you been up to?'

Her mother sounded shocked. 'Darling Roly, up to? What do you mean? I was telling that nice Brigadier of yours about the aunts—he and Dr Soames came to tea and ate almost all of one of my cakes…where was I? Oh, yes—and Constantijn came along to fetch them—he finished the cake—and said he was going over to Holland and why didn't I go with him, and he made it all so easy—tickets and things, dear, then he suggested that you might like to come too and I knew you would, so I accepted on your behalf provided you could get off, and you can. Isn't it lovely, Roly?'

Augusta began, 'Mother...' but got no further because her mother was already telling her at what time to be ready the next evening and to be sure and bring her passport. 'And don't worry if you haven't any money, darling—your father has given me plenty.'

'And how do we get back?' asked Augusta.

'Didn't I say? Constantijn has to come back early in the week—he says any day will suit him. I'll give him a ring now and tell him that everything is arranged. 'Bye, darling.' Her mother hung up before she could reply, and she went back to her chilling tea, looking thoughtful. Life, it seemed, was nothing but a series of coincidences—only her wishful thinking could possibly make anything else of it and that was because she was in love with Constantijn. After all, what was more natural than for him to go over to Holland for a weekend? It was his home and his work was there; and what could be more natural than that he should offer her mother a seat in his car when he knew she would like to go to Alkmaar? She poured away her undrinkable tea and refilled it from the pot, then bit into a bun before embarking on answering the questions being shot at her from her companions at the tea-table. When she had finished, one of the girls who had been on the tennis court when Constantijn had come to see her said, 'Gussie, what a chance for you!'

'Doing what?' Augusta wanted to know, and was greeted with a gale of laughter and an offer from several of the young ladies lolling round the table, to take her place. 'What will you wear?' asked a voice, and triggered off an earnest discussion which wasn't satisfactorily concluded by the time they went back on the wards, and when she got off duty that evening her room was quickly filled with the same young ladies, offering advice, the loan of various garments, and picking over her wardrobe with an interest worthy of a mother getting a child off to school for the first time.

She was putting the last few odds and ends into a small case when Winnie, the elderly maid who, rumour had it, had been looking after the nurses in the Home since Queen Mary had opened it, knocked on the door and told her to be quick, do, because there was a posh gent in the hall waiting for her.

'He's not posh, he's a doctor,' said Augusta, peevish because her hair hadn't gone as she had intended and she wasn't sure if the new trouser suit was really quite her after all. It was too late to do anything about it now, however. She gave Winnie a half finished box of chocolates, said, 'Here, Winnie—I've left the soft centres for you, be a darling and make my bed,' and skipped downstairs.

Constantijn was making himself agreeable to the warden, an elderly Teutonic lady with a Wagnerian manner and a heart of gold concealed beneath a massive bosom. She looked up as Augusta crossed the hall and said in an English she had never quite mastered, 'She is here—you will now go away and be content.' She beamed at Augusta and nodded delightedly, as though she had waved some sort of a wand and created some wonderful situation to make them all happy. 'You are pleasant in the trousers, Staff Nurse Brown.' Augusta went pink, avoided Constantijn's eye and said, 'Oh, Valky!' and then rather haughtily to the doctor, 'I hope I haven't kept you waiting?' She looked at him and found him smiling.

'My dear Augusta, even if you had, I should find it well worth while, for you are indeed pleasant in the trousers.' He took her case from her, spoke briefly and pleasantly to the warden in her own language, and shepherded Augusta through the door. He paused on the step. 'Why Valky?' he asked mildly.

Augusta felt pleasure at his company stealing over her; it was always the same; she felt so completely at ease with him, as though she had known him for ever and ever. 'She's German,' she explained. 'You know—the Valkyrie,' she went on with a fine disregard for the clarity of her explanation, 'Brunnhilde and all that, and no one could pronounce her name, and with a bosom like that, so she's called Valky.'

He laughed. 'Of course. I only have to be with you for a few minutes, Roly darling, and the world becomes the most amusing place.' She flashed him a bright green glance and he added, 'No, not you—I never laugh at you.'

'Why do you call me Roly?' she demanded.

He raised his eyebrows. 'Don't you want to know why I call you darling?' he murmured. Augusta said 'No' with a certain breathlessness and went down the steps and across the pavement to where the Rolls was waiting with her mother in it, smiling at her from the back seat.

Obedient to the pressure of Constantijn's hand on her arm, she got into the front of the car, received a maternal kiss on one cheek, assured her parent that she had her passport safe in her handbag and turned to meet Constantijn's amused eyes as he got in beside her.

'How very fortunate that you should be free this weekend, Augusta—we're going by Harwich, by the way.' He glanced over his shoulder. 'Shall we decide about a meal later, Mrs Brown? We don't want to cut it too fine; we can always eat on board.'

He let in the clutch and slipped into the stream of traffic. It was slow going until they were clear of the city, but once they met the A12 they made short work of the miles, for there were long stretches where the needle spun to seventy and stayed there. Augusta watched the country rush past while her mother and Constantijn, apparently unnoticing of her silence, carried on a gentle conversation which she found very soothing, so much so that she went to sleep and didn't waken until they were running into Colchester.

'There must be something about me which induces sleep,' Constantijn murmured as she sat up, feeling guilty. She said, stammering a little:

'I'm so sorry—I suppose I was tired.' She looked back at her mother, who smiled and said, 'Poor old Roly—it's my fault for rushing you like this,' and Constantijn said just as kindly, 'You've wakened at just the right moment. We're going to stop at the George for dinner—we've made very good time, and there are only nineteen miles to go.'

The hotel was old; she and her mother wandered into its courtyard while he parked the car, and admired the vine before going off together with a promise to meet him in the bar in five minutes. Which gave Augusta no time at all to ask her mother any questions.

They dined lightheartedly off oysters, steak chasseur and Crême Waflen, a delicate concoction of strawberries and cream laced with brandy and encased in a light-as-air sponge, and washed these delights down with a vintage claret, the effect of which, combined with the brandy in the pudding and the dry Martini she had had before dinner, was such as to convince Augusta that as there was nothing she could do about the situation she found herself in, she might as well enjoy herself.

Her nap had refreshed her, so much so, that when later on in the evening they were on board and on the point of departure, her mother suggested she might like an early night, she declined. They were sharing a rather splendid cabin with beds instead of bunks; she had inspected it earlier and asked her mother a little uneasily if it wasn't rather expensive, to which her mother replied that she hadn't the least idea—Constantijn had kindly arranged everything and doubtless her father would settle with him. Now, watching her mother's back disappearing cabinwards, Augusta said awkwardly, 'Our cabin is much nicer than we usually have—I suppose there weren't any others left?' She wasn't looking at him and didn't see him smile. 'I suppose there weren't,' he agreed mildly. 'Shall we walk round the deck, or do you like to stand and watch the last of England?'

She chose the latter. They stood side by side, watching Harwich growing dim and small in the not quite dark of the summer evening, and when there was no more to be seen, they strolled around the deck until she decided to go to bed. He wished her goodnight in a detached, friendly fashion which she found rather damping, he might have been a good-natured cousin or even a brother.

They breakfasted, rather grandly, at the Hotel des Indes in The Hague because Constantijn assured them that he was quite unable to drive on an empty stomach. They spoke, by tacit consent, in Dutch, and Augusta, being careful of verbs and tenses, envied her mother her easy flow of that language; probably that was why they had become such good friends.

They were in Alkmaar shortly after ten o'clock, and Augusta, more aware of Constantijn than she cared to admit, heaved a small unconscious sigh as he allowed the big car to whisper to a halt before her aunts' house. He didn't move or speak for a moment and she studied his hands lying idle on the wheel—large, kindly hands, and gentle too. He said quietly, 'Well—the end of our journey, and I for one am sorry.' He gave her a quick glance and caught her looking at him, so that she said inadequately, 'Yes—I'm sorry too.'

There were a great many things she would have liked to say; she stared at him instead so that he said, still very quiet, 'Your eyes have a great deal more to say than that pretty mouth of yours, Augusta Brown.' He smiled and she caught her breath and turned her head sharply away as her mother said, 'You'll come in, Constantijn, won't you? When I telephoned Tante Marijna she said that I was to be sure and see that you did, even if only for a minute.'

The aunts were in the little room at the end of the passage, just as they had been when Augusta had visited them so short a time before. They were sitting at the table in the same chairs, wearing, apparently, the self-same clothes. Tante Marijna looked a little more fragile perhaps, but her voice was resolute enough as she and Tante Emma greeted them. Maartje, bustling in with coffee and Jan Hagel biscuits, confided to the doctor *sotto voce* that everything was going well. 'Indeed it is,' said Tante Marijna, whose hearing was sharper than many women of half her age—an asset which she didn't scruple to use when it suited her. 'All the same, Constantijn, I should be glad if you will give me an examination.'

'Yes, of course. Will tomorrow suit you—about this time? Stay in bed will you, it will be easier for both of us. And now, if you will forgive me—my partner is going away until Sunday evening and I must see him before he goes.'

He got up and the three elder ladies bade him goodbye and at the same time urged Augusta to see him to the door.

On the step: 'You'll be here tomorrow morning?' he wanted to know.

'Oh, yes, I expect so, though I suppose I shall do the shopping—the aunts consider it good for my Dutch.'

'Ah, well,' he said carelessly, 'possibly I'll see you,' and went without another word. She stood behind the closed door, listening to the car's almost soundless departure, a prey to disappointment; she had expected him to say more than that—it was annoying that whenever she had steeled herself to resist his blandishments, he made none.

She was given the shopping to do in the morning, just as she had expected, but by being slow with her breakfast and then mislaying various articles, she contrived to be still in the house when he arrived, to be met with an offhand 'Hullo, Augusta, still here? I thought you would have been out bargaining with the shopkeepers by now.'

Augusta made a small cross sound, snatched up her basket and went, leaving a distinct impression of ill temper behind her, but her temper improved presently; it was a glorious morning even though the wind from the North Sea was blowing—as it always did blow, winter and summer alike; and the little town sparkled in the sunshine, its pavements crowded with tourists strolling along with time on their hands, while housewives, with no time at all, bustled in and out of the shops with their loaded baskets. On her way back, her shopping completed, Constantijn passed her—he was driving the Mini and she told herself that he couldn't have stopped anyway, as he would be on his morning visits, and in any case, after his offhand greeting that morning, she couldn't have cared less.

The rest of the day was spent soberly. She was entertained to a detailed account of Tante Marijna's condition—which was excellent—a good deal of local gossip, and the news that Constantijn's brother had left with Johanna for Paris during the previous week. 'So now Constantijn is alone once more,' remarked Tante Marijna, 'although I believe Susan is coming over in a week or so.'

Her mother appeared to know all about Susan. She nodded understandingly and said, 'How glad he'll be when she's decided where she wants it to be.'

Augusta bent over the wool she was untangling for Tante Emma, longing to ask questions but afraid that if she did, it might look as though she was far too interested; she had seen her mother's look in the car. Instead, she was forced to try and solve the mystery herself with such a lack of success that she was still pondering it when she went to bed that night.

They went to church in the morning, slowly walking the short distance through a great ringing of bells from the variety of churches which surrounded them. They were about to go in the church door when Augusta saw Constantijn in his little car again, but he didn't see her; for once he was driving slowly and she had time to see that he looked tired. Probably a baby case, she thought, which had kept him up most of the night. She hoped that his nice Jannie had a good breakfast waiting for him. His welfare occupied her thoughts, regrettably, during the entire morning service.

After *Koffietafel* she sat in the drawing room, looking through some old albums of long-dead Van den Pols and listening to her mother's amusing account of the Jumble Sale. Maartje had the afternoon off; at three o'clock precisely, Augusta brought up the tea tray, put the teapot on the little china box with the nightlight in it, and helped her mother pass round the fragile little cups; they were accompanied by a little dish of chocolates, because the aunts liked to keep their old-fashioned ways. It was warm in the drawing room; she would have liked to have gone for a walk, but their visit was a short one and she didn't like to hurt the old ladies' feelings by implying that she was bored. And so she was, she admitted to herself, and felt ashamed at the thought. To make up for it, she went down to the kitchen presently, having offered to get the evening meal ready. Maartje would cook it when she returned, but it would help her considerably if she put the chicken in the oven and prepared the salad. It was cooler in the kitchen, for she had opened the door as well as a window and stood in the cool breeze arranging lettuce and tomatoes and chicory in a cut glass bowl, she was standing back the better to

admire her efforts when she heard the front door
bang. That would be Maartje. She washed her hands,
tidied the kitchen and went upstairs again. Constantijn
was in the drawing room, leaning, very large, against
the chimney-piece. As she went in her mother said:

'There you are, Roly,' and Augusta frowned. Of
course she was there, and she really would have to
remind her dear mother not to keep calling her by
that stupid name. 'Constantijn's waiting to take you
out,' went on Mrs Brown, ignoring the frown, her
voice backed by a gently chorused 'Won't that be
nice?' from the aunts. Very nice, she thought crossly,
if she were asked. She shot him a smouldering look
across the room and he left the mantelpiece, took her
arm, said pleasantly to the room's occupants: 'Excuse
us, won't you?' and pushed her gently out of the door
again and closed it behind them. In the passage he
said, 'You're quite an eyeful when you seethe, Augusta. I didn't ask you before, because if I had you
would have had time to think up some splendid ex-
cuses, and if I had known that you were in the kitchen
I would have gone straight there and whisked you off,
apron and all.' He smiled suddenly at her and her
treacherous heart took command. 'Come out to dinner,' he wheedled. 'I've had a busy weekend.'

She found herself smiling back at him, idiotically
incapable of anything else. 'I'll be ten minutes,' she
promised—in which time she achieved a great deal;
re-did her face, brushed her hair, changed her shoes
and tights, sprayed her person discreetly with Hou-
bigant's Chantilly, and then, more or less satisfied
with her appearance, ran downstairs to the drawing
room to say goodbye.

The Rolls was at the door, and as she got in beside

him he asked, 'You won't mind if we go home first? Van den Post, my partner, intends to ring me back about something—it won't take long.'

Augusta didn't mind in the least. Just being with him wherever it was was sufficient; she probably wouldn't see him for a long time—perhaps never— once this weekend was over and they were back in London, and once there, she promised herself, she would allow her common sense to master the dream world she was living in at the moment. They went into his house, and Jannie came bustling to meet them, looking put out.

'There,' she said, 'the moment you'd gone, Doctor, that boy came knocking at the door and what could I do but let him in, poor lad. Such a nasty cut on his hand and bleeding all over my nice clean floors. He's in the surgery and I hope I did right—he wasn't in a fit state to be sent on to Dr van den Post and you said you'd be back.' She smiled belatedly and warmly at Augusta and added, 'Good day, Miss Brown, it is nice to see you again.'

Augusta would have echoed her sentiments, but Constantijn gave her no time; with her hand fast held in his he crossed the hall to the door which led to the surgery. 'Perhaps you'll give me a hand,' he remarked placidly. 'What is it you say in English—Sing for your supper? You shall have the opportunity of doing just that.'

The surgery, built unobtrusively on to the side of the old house, was a fair size and well equipped. The patient, a boy of twelve or so, was sitting on a wooden chair with his hand wrapped in a towel which bore ample testimony to the fact that his hand was badly cut indeed. 'There's an apron behind the door,' said the doctor, and took off his coat.

Augusta put the rubber apron on, taking a large reef in its length and wrapping it around her small waist; the result was bulky but adequate. While she did it her eyes were busy searching for the more obvious things they would need—instruments on the trolley, the dressings bin, a glass-fronted cupboard with its complement of first aid necessities. She flipped a paper towel from the neat pile laid ready and put it on the examination couch as Constantijn sat the boy close to lay his arm upon it. The cut was deep, across the palm of his hand, and the hand was dirty. Augusta cleaned it up with swabs and Savlon solution and then stood back to watch while Constantijn stooped to examine it. 'How did you do it?' he inquired.

'Billhook,' the boy answered briefly.

'Did you tell anyone at home?' queried the doctor. The boy flushed. 'No.'

'What were you doing? Fooling about with friends?' The boy nodded. 'Well, you'll have to tell your mother about it when you get home. I'm going to put some stitches in it now and give you an injection, and tomorrow you must come to morning surgery. You understand?' He looked at Augusta. 'There are needles in the covered dish on the trolley, and some skin sutures—take the lid off for me, will you? he'll have to have ATS too, it's in the corner cupboard and the needles and syringes are in the drawer below.'

She pottered about happily enough under his placid directions, drawing up the local anaesthetic, handing things, clearing up, and when the boy, neatly strapped up, had been dispatched kitchenwards for a cup of coffee from the motherly Jannie, and she was disentangling herself from the apron, Constantijn came across the surgery to help her. 'So, Miss Brown, you are as capable as you are pretty.' He threw the apron into a corner and she went and picked it up and put it in the sink to be washed.

'Look at you,' she scolded, 'and why will you call me Miss Brown?'

He put his handsome head on one side and studied her. 'Well, I think because you are old-fashioned in a charming way. Oh, I don't mean clothes and make-up and such-like female nonsense. But I'll not call you that if you dislike it. What shall it be? Augusta? Roly? Darling?'

He was laughing at her, she went a furious pink and flounced to the door. 'Augusta will do very well,' she said stiffly. 'Roly is a silly name and—and...'

'Darling?' he prompted from behind her. She put a hand out to open the door and had it gripped gently in one of his. She wasn't sure if he turned her round to face him or whether she had done it of her own free will, all that she knew was that she was fast in his arms and he was going to kiss her. The sensible part of her mind warned her sternly not to encourage him; she nudged it on one side as she lifted her face to his.

Presently, when she had her breath again and her heart had steadied its furious pounding, she said almost shyly, 'Constantijn, we mustn't—because of Susan.'

He took her by the shoulders and held her back a little so that he could see her face. His own was faintly puzzled. 'Susan? Now why on earth...?'

'Well, you're going to marry her,' said Augusta in

a stony little voice. She saw the twitch come and go at the corner of his mouth; if he were to laugh she wouldn't be able to bear it. He didn't laugh but said in a matter-of-fact voice, 'I can't think where you got that from, my dear girl. Susan is my ward.'

Augusta's eyes became green saucers. 'Your ward? But you're too young!'

He smiled. 'It's very simple—her father asked my father to be her guardian when and if he died—she was twelve when he did and my own father died a year later and passed her on to me. I was twenty-four then. Now she is almost twenty-one and I am thirty-three.'

Augusta stared up into his face. 'But did you never want to marry her? She's so beautiful,' and was shaken by his honesty when he said, 'Oh yes—a year or so ago—but it never came to anything.' She watched the twinkle come into his eyes. 'Have I shocked you? But you did want to know, didn't you, and I can't think how that's possible, for after all, you cast me for a villain right from the first moment we met, didn't you?'

Augusta pushed against his chest with one hand and he loosed her at once, which she discovered wasn't at all what she wanted. 'I didn't cast you for anything,' she remonstrated. 'I didn't know anything about you, only it seemed obvious…I mean you were always with Susan, and—and…'

He took her in his arms again. There was a gleam in his eyes, but his voice was quiet and unhurried. 'Dear Roly, empty your carroty head of the nonsense you've chosen to fill it with. You must know by now that I've fallen more than a little in love with you, but you're not one to be hurried, are you, and I can wait for what I want. But this is to remind you.'

He bent his head and kissed her again; a gentle kiss that cherished her and kept her safe and at the same time gave her a very good idea of how exciting it was to be kissed by the right man. He released her with the same gentleness, saying in a quite different voice:

'I thought we'd go to Oegstgeest for dinner. There's a rather good place there—de Beukenhof—it's less than an hour's run.' He glanced at his watch. 'Van den Post should telephone at any moment.'

Augusta, a little breathless still, said, 'That sounds lovely—the dinner, I mean. I'll go and wait somewhere, shall I?'

He went with her across the hall and ushered her into the drawing room and went back to the surgery as the telephone began to ring. Left to herself, Augusta went, naturally enough, to the elegant mirror on one wall and studied herself closely. She looked the same, which was surprising as she felt quite different inside. She smiled at her reflected face, refurbished her lipstick, did things to her hair and, satisfied, began a slow tour of the room. When she had been there before she hadn't been able to observe it closely, but now she was alone... She began with the portraits—rather severe family ones, she supposed, in heavy frames. Several of the gentlemen among them exhibited the same faintly hawk nose which Constantijn had undoubtedly inherited from them; the pale eyes too were disconcertingly like his. She studied the women next, none of them beauties, which was surprising, for these bygone men were surely handsome enough to be able to take their pick of contemporary lovelies. She stood staring at a brown mouse of a

woman, richly dressed in the style of the Second
Empire, and wearing splendid jewels, and wearing, as
well, the satisfied appearance of a well-loved, well-
cosseted wife. Perhaps they liked their women plain.
Was that why Constantijn loved her? She chuckled
happily and then jumped as he said from behind her,
'Why do you smile at my Great-great-aunt Emma?
She was a very charming woman, so I've been told.'

Augusta turned round to look at him. 'I didn't hear
you come in,' she observed, 'and I wasn't laughing
at her—only at a thought. The men are all so handsome and the women are a little—well, plain.'

He put a hand under her chin and lifted her face to
study it intently. 'Beauty is in the eye of the beholder,' he quoted softly, 'and I could enlarge on that
theme, but I won't at the moment.' He took his hand
away and took her arm instead and walked her to the
door. 'I shall have to do a certain amount of work
tomorrow, but I shall be free at midday for a couple
of hours. Perhaps all of you will come here for lunch
and I can show you the rest of the house.'

Augusta turned a glowing face to his. 'Oh, that
would be super—I'm sure they'll all love to come.'
She paused, frowning. 'Shall we be back in time this
evening to ask them?'

'No.' He sounded very positive about it. 'But you
could broach the subject in the morning—better still,
I'll write a note and you can let them have it.'

This knotty problem solved, they went out to the
car and a few minutes later were streaking down the
main road, south to Leiden, Oegstgeest and dinner.

Augusta, lying in bed much later, tried happily to
remember every minute of the evening—it had been
wonderful, although Constantijn had made no further

reference to the future. They had talked a great deal, but not about themselves, and they had laughed a great deal too. The food had been delicious although she hadn't much idea of what she had eaten, and afterwards they had driven back to Alkmaar and she had gone to his house with him while he wrote a note to the aunts.

When they finally reached her aunts' house it was very late indeed, but her mother, dressing-gowned and yawning, had opened the door to them, hoping, sleepily, that they had enjoyed their evening and inviting them to drink coffee in the kitchen if they had a mind to. She then wished them a drowsy goodnight and disappeared upstairs, and they had spent another half hour sitting by the Aga in the kitchen talking while their coffee cooled, and when, at last, they had wished each other goodnight at the door, Constantijn had kissed her once again—a quick friendly kiss, not at all like the others, but he had looked at her as though the kiss were something other than it was and she had gone to bed happy, knowing that there was still a great deal they had to know of each other but that it would be a delight to find out. She slept at length and didn't wake until she heard Maartje going quietly downstairs in the early morning.

The lunch party was everything it should have been. Augusta, who was beginning to know Constantijn, wasn't surprised to find the food superb and the table appointments of great elegance, for he was a man who wasn't prepared to settle for less than perfection if it were obtainable. The room they lunched in was of a fair size with a beautiful plaster ceiling and panelled walls of dark wood and furnished with period pieces of the William and Mary era. The sideboard displayed a good deal of silver of the same period and a glass-fronted cabinet along one wall housed a collection of engraved glass goblets. The portraits of even more van Lindemann ancestors, of whom there seemed to be a great number, stared at them from above the panelling as they ate their way through scrambled eggs with salmon, Mirabeau steak and a lemon cream which Augusta rightly deduced hadn't come out of a packet. They drank a wine she didn't recognize and she was too shy to ask, but it had the happy effect of allowing her to rise from the table feeling very slightly lightheaded, although she concluded that there might be other reasons for this pleasurable sensation.

The aunts were escorted to the drawing room and left, at their own request, to digest the delicacies they had just eaten, while Constantijn escorted Augusta and her mother round the house. It took quite some time, for they didn't hurry, but paused to examine a couple of small paintings by Avercamp which Augusta liked very much, and several pen and ink drawings by Jan Breugel the elder, as well as a flower study by Ambrosius Bosschaert. There was a great deal of porcelain to examine as well and a collection of silver. Augusta would have liked to have spent a great deal more time looking at everything, but she remembered that Constantijn had said that he had work to do in the afternoon, and they were due to leave that very evening so she said a little reluctantly,

'It's all most interesting and beautiful and I could spend hours...but we do have to pack, Mother, and I'm sure Constantijn has things to do.' She caught her mother's eye with a compelling glance, causing that lady to lay down a Louis XV snuffbox she was examining and remark, 'Goodness, so we have. You'll forgive us if we go, Constantijn?'

He drove them back in the Rolls, Augusta beside him, and as he drew up before the house he gave her a sidelong glance and said warmly,

'Thank you, Augusta—what a tactful and thoughtful wife you will make.' He had spoken quietly so that she had barely heard him, which didn't prevent her blushing so hotly that Tante Emma, getting out carefully between them, glanced at her niece and remarked that the dear child had an unusually high colour.

It was on their journey back that Augusta asked diffidently if he was going to remain in England or returning to Holland, and when he replied carelessly that he would be going back to Alkmaar within a few days but that he would be in London again shortly, she forbore from commenting further, sensing that, for some reason or other, he didn't want to discuss it. And later, when they arrived at St Jude's and she had bidden her mother goodbye and was standing with him in the entrance to the Nurses' Home, he said merely, '*Tot ziens*, my dear girl, it was a pleasant weekend,' and she bit her lip, for it wasn't quite what she had expected. All the same, she said in a composed voice, 'Yes, wasn't it? Thanks for taking us, Constantijn.' She put out her hand, to have it engulfed and held for a brief moment before she took her bag from him and went inside.

Upstairs in her room, changing back into her familiar uniform, she wondered why he had been so casual, and not finding a satisfactory answer, persuaded herself that he was probably a man who hated being demonstrative in public.

CHAPTER SEVEN

THE NEXT FEW DAYS were long and hot and busy, and even if she had wanted to think a great deal about Constantijn there was little time to do so, and that, Augusta admitted to herself, was probably a good thing.

She had half expected to hear from him, as indeed she did, in the form of a delicately arranged bouquet of sweet peas which arrived for her on the day after her return to St Jude's, but the card which accompanied it was disappointingly cool, bearing only the words, Yours, C. However, the flowers, displayed in various vessels around her room, called forth a great deal of interesting comment from her friends, and she put the card, businesslike though it was, under her pillow...for had he not said that he loved her a little?

It was on her fourth day back that the telephone rang as she was returning from Staff Nurses' supper. Sister had gone for her weekend, it had been a busy day for it had been the first day of 'take-in', so that three of the five empty beds in the ward had already been filled. Augusta lifted the receiver, already busy planning which patient was well enough to be boarded out in another ward for the night so that she would have another empty bed. It was Archie, sounding for once serious.

'Gussie? There's a flap on—a block of flats has collapsed, somewhere down by the docks. We're the nearest hospital, though we should be able to move some of the cases on once we've seen what they are. All the same we're going to be busy. The big brass will be in presently, in the meantime get some empty beds, will you? The accident ward's no dice—they're full.'

'I've two empties and I can get six more down the centre—Medical can take some of our up cases for the night...who shall I send over?' She thought rapidly. 'Mr Wills could go; he's a simple dressing, and Jimmy Short and Clarke and Tippett...that'll give us twelve beds.'

'Good. Get on with it right away, will you? The RSO'll be up to see you some time.'

She put the receiver down and picked it up again immediately because it rang once more. It was Matron this time. 'Staff Nurse Brown? All day nurses have been recalled to their wards—you can expect them back shortly. Borrow any equipment they can spare from the accident ward and let me know if you are in difficulties. An Office Sister will be round presently.'

Augusta said, 'Yes, Matron,' then telephoned in her turn to Men's Medical, the porter's lodge, the linen room...she put the telephone down finally as Miss Hawkes, one of the Office Sisters, came into the ward.

'I'll need some dressing packs,' began Augusta without preamble. 'I've enough to cover the night, but not for an emergency. Is there anyone in CSSD yet, Miss Hawkes?'

'There will be in a few minutes. Let me have a list—I'll see you get them. What about bed linen? How many beds can you manage?'

Augusta told her. 'And I've got Nurse Hobbs and Nurse Gibbs here—they're getting the men transferred to Medical. We can get their beds made up while the porters are putting up the spares.'

Miss Hawkes nodded. 'You realise that you may have to stay on duty until things settle down?'

Augusta said that yes, she did, thinking privately that it was the silliest question she had had to answer for a long time…still, poor old Hawkie, it was part of her job to ask questions, however silly.

They were almost ready when the first case came up. They had all made beds with an urgency inspired by the singsong sirens of the ambulances as they came and went. The nurses had returned long since and they had worked like beavers, for it wasn't only beds—there were trolleys to be laid up, vacoliters of plasma to be arranged where they could be grabbed at once, forms laid out ready to be snatched, linen to be stacked, dressing packets to be piled in such good order that no one would need to fumble around. The night staff had come on duty too, and Augusta had to stop for ten precious minutes to give the report before they took over their normal duties in the ward, for despite the emergency, the patients still needed their usual care and treatment.

The RSO had paid a brief visit too. He was a tall be-spectacled man from Mombasa; as black as coal, brilliantly clever and rejoicing in the name of George England, he never appeared to hurry and nonetheless contrived to be where he was wanted most. He was one of the most popular men in the hospital. He said now, 'Hullo, Gussie,' and because there was no time to waste: 'Ninety families in the flats—one end's caved in. Our team's down there now—there'll be a dozen more as well. The idea's to send the ortho-paedic cases straight to Duke's and the head injuries to Maple Cross—the rest will be split up, so heaven knows what we'll get. We'll try and let you know before we send the patients up, but don't blow your top if something comes up unannounced. Got plenty of staff?'

'You must be joking,' Augusta said cheerfully, 'not that it makes any difference; we'll manage, like everyone else.'

He nodded and grinned. 'I'll be in the accident room or at least they'll find me if you should want me, but keep it to the urgents, won't you? Sir will be in too.' Sir was Mr Rogers, the senior consultant surgeon, a middle-aged man of deceptively meek appearance and a voice like a sergeant-major when things went wrong. Augusta lifted her eyebrows in mock dismay and flew back into the ward to harry the porters; there were still three more beds to put up.

The patients came after that, in a slow steady trickle and in various states of disablement. By one o'clock in the morning two of them had died, three had gone to Theatre and were now lying, surrounded by post-operative equipment—drainage tubes, suction pumps and the like—fighting, albeit unconsciously, for their lives, unaware that the nurses were fighting even harder. The rest of the admissions had a fair chance of pulling through, or so it seemed, and Augusta sent two nurses to make up the vacated beds once more, for ICU was full, and Archie, on a quick visit half an hour earlier, had said that there were still cases coming in, some of them pretty grotty. George England had appeared too in his theatre gown and boots, and taken a quick look at the casualties.

'Managing?' he wanted to know laconically.

Augusta, hot and untidy and notwithstanding, cool

and alert said, 'Yes, George, very nicely, thank you.'
As she was—she had been sent three more nurses and
while there was a mountain of work to do, they were
getting through it. Most of the admissions were in a
state of shock, and while some of them were silent
and uncaring of what was happening around them
there were several who were restless and irritable.
Presently and in turn they would go to Theatre, but
for the time being they lay, most of them on blood
transfusions and most of them too with their senses
dimmed with morphia or pethedine. The nurses went
quietly to and fro, adjusting drips, repacking wounds,
moistening lips that weren't allowed to drink, doing
the hundred and one jobs that never came to an end,
and Augusta going to and fro with them, working as
hard—even harder, for she had the responsibility.
When Matron came to the ward, it was with the welcome news that coffee and sandwiches had been organised for the nurses so that they could go one by
one as they could be spared and swallow and munch
hurriedly in the ward kitchen. Archie, busy over a
patient who had collapsed, said cheerfully, 'Ha! Must
keep the lamps burning, eh?' His little joke made
them all laugh as the first nurse hummed gleefully to
the kitchen. Augusta, syphoning a stomach tube, said,
'Five minutes each, one at a time,' and on the same
breath, 'Where's Sir, Archie? Surely not in the accident room?'

He was drawing up methedrine. 'Lord, no, he's
been in Theatre…brought reinforcements with him
too; means George can be on the spot if he's wanted.
Old Halliday is in the other theatre and they're doing
as much small stuff as they can downstairs.' He in-
serted the needle into a flaccid vein. 'There's a couple

more to come up—ruptured spleen and a nasty lacerated face.'

Augusta tidied their mess with methodical haste and prepared to move on to the next patient. She glanced at the clock; it was almost three; she would ask, as soon as she could spare a minute, if two of the nurses could go to bed as soon as the two new patients were admitted. Someone would have to carry on once the day started; there were several part-time nurses due in and one or two nursing aides, but most of the patients needed skilled treatment and there wouldn't be enough nurses on duty to go round. She was still puzzling it out when Matron appeared again, looking pretty and not in the least tired. Augusta, conscious of a strong desire to yawn, went to meet her.

'You have two more coming up, I believe, Staff Nurse. Send your third year nurse to bed and one of the juniors as soon as you can, will you?' She eyed Augusta thoughtfully. 'I expect Sister will return as soon as possible. Until she does, or I can find someone to replace you, do you feel able to stay on duty? There will be a warm meal very shortly—you must take time off for that. Send your nurses as you think fit. You have Nurse Stevens with you, haven't you? She's senior enough to be left for a short time.' She paused. 'No, perhaps not—I'll see that something hot is sent up to the kitchen for you, just in case you are needed urgently.'

Augusta brightened at the mention of food, for now that she came to think about it she was very hungry, and she imagined the other nurses were too. She thanked Matron with the warmth of anticipation and was told briskly to go away and get on with whatever she had been doing. Both patients had been warded

by the time the last of the nurses returned from their
hot meal; Augusta gobbled down a bowl of soup, but
didn't dare start on the eggs and chips keeping hot
for her, for the man with the ruptured spleen was in
a bad way—he would be going to Theatre as soon as
the second litre of blood had run in. The man who
had come up with him—the one with the severe face
lacerations—was quite young and powerfully built
and lay quietly staring at the ceiling. Augusta had
been surprised to find his right arm heavily bandaged
above the elbow and as she lifted it gently on to a
pillow she said, 'The doctor will be up presently—I
can't give you a drink until he's been in case you
have to have something more done. Does it hurt very
much?'

He shook his head and winced at the movement.
His face had been stitched and the stitches sprayed
with Nobecutane so that it looked like a patchwork
quilt. 'I'm OK,' he said a little thickly, 'but I don't
like this thing.' His eyes turned to his other arm, attached by needle and tubing to the drip at the side of
the bed.

'Oh, that'll be coming down in next to no time,'
said Augusta comfortably. 'You lost quite a lot of
blood—this is the quickest way of getting it back inside you.' She had a quiet hand on his wrist, taking
his pulse. It was much too rapid, although he looked
all right. All the same, before she went to a patient
at the other end of the ward she warned Nurse Meek
to keep an eye on him. Archie would be up in a few
minutes to explain the bandaged arm; after all, they
had told her not to expect details at once if they were
pushed and the case wasn't desperate.

She had just changed a drip when something, some

faint sound probably, made her look round. The man she had just left was sitting up in bed tearing with his bandaged arm at the tube attached to the vacoliter. She started down the ward moving fast, but not fast enough—she was several beds away from him when he succeeded in pulling it out so that the blood poured from the vacoliter as the tubing swung free. Worse, the man was tugging at his bandage despite the efforts of Nurse Meek.

In the ensuing confusion, Augusta found time to feel sorry for her—she had only been out of training school a week; until that night the only blood she had seen had been theoretical—the vacoliter had been half empty, but its contents were sufficient to make a spectacular display; Nurse Meek made a small gasping sound and flaked out at Augusta's feet. 'Good grief!' said Augusta, thoroughly exasperated, and spared a few seconds to make sure she was all right. Apparently she was, for she opened her eyes, smiled with hazy apology and turned on to her side to fall immediately asleep. Augusta stepped over her and ran to the other side of the bed just as the man dragged off the last of the bandage. 'Leave your dressing alone,' she said breathlessly and without any result whatever, for he brushed her hand away as though it had been gossamer and pulled the dressing off too, exposing a jagged wound just above the elbow—it had, she saw, been stitched, but probably a ligature round one of the blood vessels had slipped its knot, for it was bleeding fast.

The patient looked at her with the faraway expression which conveyed to her the unfortunate possibility of concussion which had been delayed or an unsuspected subaranoid—it really didn't matter which, she thought wearily; he was going to be a handful. She gave up the unequal struggle to cover the wound, but concentrated on getting two fingers over the brachial artery and applying pressure, and was presently rewarded by the sight of the lessened bleeding. She would only have to hold on for a minute or two—Stevens had gone to Theatre to collect a patient; Stebbings had gone down for a well-earned tea break; it was just sheer bad luck that old Tom in one of the side wards should have fallen out of his bed not five minutes earlier and both night nurses were engaged in hauling him back in again—and poor Meek—she cast a quick look over the bed and saw that she was still sleeping, looking very comfortable despite the hard floor. She was even snoring gently. Augusta turned her attention to her patient and said sharply, 'Oh no, you don't, laddie!' as he swung his other arm across, missing her swiftly ducked head by an inch or so. She had her back to the door so that she couldn't look round when she heard footsteps, but she let out a relieved breath and called, not too loudly, 'Stevens? Leave that trolley and telephone Archie or the RSO—anyone—and get them up here fast!'

'Will I do?' said Mr Rogers from behind her. He was still in his green theatre gown and cap and looked so ill-tempered and tired that she braced herself for any forthright remark he might make, at the same time aware that there was someone else behind her—a large hand came down over her shoulder and took over from her stiff fingers. 'Shall I?' inquired Constantijn, 'while you get one or two things.'

She flew to the centre of the ward, searched for the packs she needed; added it to the trolley she had laid in expectation of just such an emergency as this one and whisked it back to the bed, the while her tired brain strove to wrestle with the problem of Constantijn being there. Sir was mumbling away to himself, but he stopped when she pushed the trolley close to him and said merely, 'H'm—slipped ligature, I suppose—looks like an intercranial pressure too...' He mumbled some more and then said, 'This is Doctor van Lindemann—he was dining with me—brought him along to give a hand.'

Augusta was unwrapping forceps and retractors and needles and gut; she did it neatly, without touching anything but their outside wrappings. She said briefly, 'We've met—you'll need the lamp, won't you?' and went, rather leaden-footed, to fetch it. She hadn't dared to look at Constantijn yet because she had the absurd notion that if she did she might throw herself into his arms and burst into tears—she was still feeling lightheaded from his sudden, unexpected appearance. The patient had become quieter; Constantijn was fastening a tourniquet above the wound and holding him still without much effort. Against her better judgment Augusta looked at him; he smiled and she smiled back and Mr Rogers said to no one in particular, 'So you know each other.'

'Very well indeed,' said Constantijn. 'If you're ready, I'll change places.'

It was a slipped ligature all right. Sir, mumbling and grumbling under his breath, found it quickly enough and set to work to repair the damage. He had straightened his back and turned to take the gut dangling from the Cheatles forceps in Augusta's hand, when his eye fell upon Nurse Meek, lying reposefully on the floor where she had fallen. He paused only for a moment and then remarked mildly, 'You work your nurses hard, Staff Nurse. Is she all right?'

Augusta put the Cheatles back in the jar; with all the superiority of five years she said: 'The poor child fainted—she's been marvellous, but she's only been out of PTS for two weeks and this is the first time she's seen anything worse than an appendicectomy scar. She's asleep. As soon as I can I'll get her to bed.'

She handed Constantijn the scissors and caught his eye; as usual he was looking amused and she went a furious scarlet and glowered at him, suddenly aware that she must look quite awful—her bow was under one ear, her cap at a ridiculous angle, and her gown was stained and filthy. She realised that Sir was speaking and made haste to beg his pardon because she hadn't heard a word. He growled, 'Why must I repeat myself? I want to know where your nurses are.'

The lift gates clanged as she answered, 'Theatre sent for someone to fetch back your last patient—the night nurses are in the side ward because old Tom fell out of bed, and there's a nurse at tea—just for ten minutes.' She hastened to add, 'And of course, there's Nurse Meek here.' She paused to push her cap straight and went on, 'There are plenty of staff, it's just that they didn't happen to be here—they'll be back any minute now.'

She was right; they were all there within seconds of each other. Mr Rogers, without looking up, said, 'Constantijn, take a look at that girl and if she's asleep—and I think she may well be—get her over to the Nurses' Home; one of the nurses can let someone or other know. And perhaps we might have a cup of tea in your kitchen, Staff Nurse Brown—you will of course join us.'

Augusta said, 'Thank you, sir,' rather absentmindedly because she was sharing out the work—they were over the worst now, she thought, but there was still a great deal to do and there wouldn't be many nurses coming on in the morning. She looked at the clock; it was morning, anyway. She watched Constantijn bending over Meek; presently he picked her up, saying, 'There's nothing wrong that I can see—she's sound asleep though. I'll carry her over to the Home—if someone could telephone now, I can hand her over.' He strode away as a nurse scuttled into the office and then went to make the tea.

Augusta hadn't thought she was tired until, at Mr Rogers' gruff bidding, she sat down in the ward kitchen. It was a small, quite cosy place, crammed with shelves of china stacked trays and with lists and notices pinned on the walls, like the one extolling the reader to be careful—in red ink—and going on to give the advice—in blue ink—that old Tom was allergic to eggs, there were diabetic diets, salt-free diets, fat-free diets; in fact the variety was unending. They were interspersed by sinister little notes conveying various warnings about broken china; the counting of teaspoons daily and the dire consequences if Sister wasn't told. Augusta, who had spent several years among similar notices on every ward kitchen in the hospital, ignored them, having indeed written some of them herself, but Sir wandered around reading them commenting adversely upon the grammar and making biting remarks about their context. He had a cup of tea in one hand and a slice of bread and butter in the other and reminded her strongly of the Mad Hatter without his hat. He turned round when Constantijn came in and remarked, 'Ah, my dear chap, this tea is excellent and I'm sure Nurse will butter you a slice of bread.' But Constantijn put a hand on her shoulder as she started to get to her feet.

'Stay where you are, Augusta, I can get it for myself. Home Sister was waiting for us; we shook Nurse Meek awake just long enough to get her upstairs.' He poured himself some tea and gave Augusta a long piercing look. 'You look fagged out,' he observed. 'How much longer will you be on duty?'

'Sister will be back about midday, Matron thinks. But I'm quite all right—I don't feel tired at all,' lied Augusta smilingly, unaware that her eyes were sunk in her head with fatigue and that she had no colour at all. Only her hair, a little wispy now, glowed rustily. It needed a tremendous effort to stand up again; the thought of the work still to be done appalled her; the temptation to sit down again was so strong that she was actually on the point of doing so when Sir said:

'Well, we'd better take a look at that spleen. Nurse, I want that lacerations case to have a skull X-ray—get young Dukes on to it.' He spoke in a voice whose briskness belied his tired face. She had perforce to follow him back into the ward where he and Constantijn became instantly engrossed in the patient, concentration wiping out the fatigue in their faces. Presently they went away. Constantijn gave her a half smile as they went but said nothing at all, a fact she barely noticed because she was up to her eyes in work. The case went to Theatre soon after that, and leaving a nurse on guard by the man with the facial injuries, Augusta tiredly disposed her little team for what she called mopping-up operations.

As the new day advanced, the nurses were replaced one by one, beginning with the most junior; the night staff had stayed on duty so that the day nurses who had been up all or most of the night could go to breakfast and take a much-needed break; the patients had been sorted out too—some had been transferred to other hospitals, some—the desperate cases—to the hard pressed ICU; some, the lucky few, were being allowed home. The hospital settled back into its regular pattern of life, while worn-out housemen shaved and took quick naps and ate breakfast before getting on with another day's work and Ward Sisters arranged and rearranged off-duty so that those who had been up all night could have at least part of the day to sleep. Matron had been up to see Augusta after breakfast and asked her again if she felt she could stay on until Sister returned. 'If you could manage to do so, Staff Nurse,' she said, 'I see no reason why you shouldn't have the rest of the day off. Most of the part-time staff nurses are willing to do extra hours for a day or so, and this should ease the situation.'

Augusta, who was feeling huffy because she hadn't seen Constantijn again—he could at least have come up to the ward, however briefly—said she wasn't in the least tired anyway and was quite prepared to stay for as long as Matron wished. That lady gave her a considered look, but all she said was, 'Thank you, Nurse.' Her calculating eye swept the ward; there were still beds down the middle and the place was cluttered with a mass of equipment, all vitally contributing to the recovery of the patients, although several of the beds were, sadly, empty now. She turned to go. 'Be sure and have a good rest when you go off duty, Staff Nurse,' she said.

Augusta, whose feet were aching and whose eyes were burning in her head, thought it very unlikely that she would wish to do anything else, for she had just eaten an enormous breakfast which had the effect of making her very sleepy. Overcome by a sudden self-pity, she gave a prodigious sniff; nothing and no one—the no one was nameless, but she meant Constantijn—would dissuade her from a long day's sleep.

Sister arrived back just after noon, and delaying only long enough to tell Augusta that she looked too terrible for words, demanded the report. It took quite a time, especially as Augusta had to explain which nurses were on duty and which were off and why poor little Meek was in bed for the day. At the end of her recital, Sister remarked:

'You look as though you could do with a day in bed yourself. Off you go, Gussie.'

She went thankfully; she would go straight to bed after a bath; she could make a cup of tea and have it in bed, but when she was ready, the effort to make tea was too great, and she got into bed, closed her eyes, and was instantly asleep.

She had, as she thought, barely closed her eyes when she was shaken awake by Millie, firmly told to sit up, and then given a cup of tea.

"'Ere, Staff, drink this nice cuppa—yer young man's waiting for yer. 'E told me ter get yer out of bed and yer were ter dress, and if yer didn't 'e'd come up 'isself, and that ain't allowed.'

Augusta, half asleep, began on the tea which revived her sufficiently for her to ask indignantly, 'What's the time? And I haven't got a young man.'

'Four o'clock, an' it's that nice doctor 'oo was 'ere before, an' I knows 'e's yer young man, 'cos 'e said so.'

Augusta thought this over while she finished her tea. 'Well, I shan't,' she said at length, pettishly. She banged the cup and saucer down on her bedtable, thumped up her pillows and prepared to lie down again. 'I will not get up,' she repeated.

'Oh, yes, yer will. 'E said—She'll not take kindly to the idea, but tell 'er that if I can, so can she.'

Augusta was by now fully awake, for Millie's voice was piercing as well as persistent. 'Oh, all right.' Part of her was furious at not being allowed to sleep, but part of her—the larger part, she had to admit—was pleasantly excited to think that Constantijn wanted to see her. She sat up again and threw back the bed-clothes and Millie coaxed her in a satisfied voice, 'There's the girl—I'll make yer bed, Staff.'

Augusta tore into her clothes; it was a very warm afternoon; she topped a minimum of undies with a sleeveless shift of a pleasing shade of pink which she mistakenly hoped would lend colour to her pale face, did her hair carefully, snatched up her handbag and flew downstairs, tiredness forgotten.

Constantijn was talking to Valky. It was annoying to see that he looked as fresh and well rested as a man who had spent the entire night in his bed; he also looked annoyingly calm, self-assured—and not in the least penitent at getting her out of bed. As she approached them, Valky said rather dramatically, 'Ah, the poor young girl—so white and tired and so over-worked.'

'As are all the nurses in the hospital,' said Constantijn casually, and Augusta, already edgy, her pleasure at the sight of him evaporating at his unfeeling attitude, glowered at him, her eyes glittering greenly.

'Which makes it all right to have me got out of bed after barely four hours' sleep...' she choked on rage.

'Quite all right.' His voice, she considered, was hatefully smooth. 'You're young and healthy and perfectly able to cope.' He smiled with charm. 'I thought—I hoped you would like to come out with me.'

Before she could think of an answer to this, he had caught her hand in his, said goodbye to the beaming Valky, and led her outside to the car. As he slid into the seat beside her, Augusta asked, 'Where are we going?' She still sounded cross.

He leaned over and kissed her lightly on a pale cheek. 'You'll see,' he said; he wasn't teasing any more—his voice sounded warm and comforting so that she felt a little ashamed of herself.

Ten minutes later he turned the car into the quiet square where Lady Belway lived and drew up before her house door. Augusta, who hadn't spoken at all throughout the short drive, took one look and burst out indignantly, 'Well, I simply will not go visiting...' and was interrupted patiently. 'My dear girl, I know you're tired, but to try to recover some of your usual good humour. Lady Belway isn't home—she's gone to Paris to see Susan because I was unable to—and a fine upheaval it was. If it hadn't been so urgent...' he sighed. 'I thought that we might have tea here, it will be quiet, and if you're going to doze, which I have no doubt at all you will, you might as well do it in peace.'

This speech had the effect of waking Augusta up.

She said quite sharply, 'I've no intention of going to sleep,' but she allowed herself to be helped out of the car and crossed the pavement to the door which was opened by Sims, the butler, who wished them a civil good afternoon and went on to say that they would be served their tea in the garden if they would be so good as to follow him.

He led the way down a passage at the back of the hall and opened a door into a room with french windows giving on to a small but charming garden where there was a table, several comfortable chairs and a canopied hammock set invitingly in the shade of two lime trees. Augusta's ill-humour dwindled away at the pleasant sight. She hurried across the small lawn, exclaiming, 'Oh, what heaven!' and was about to sink into the hammock when she stopped and turned round to say to Constantijn:

'I don't know why you bother with me—you think of such nice things and I was absolutely—absolutely wrathy.' Rather disconcertingly, he agreed, adding, 'But then there are so many things you don't know about me.'

She sat in the hammock and he took the chair opposite her. It was quite true, there were a great many things she didn't know about him; she would want to know some of them at least before she got any more involved—supposing he were to ask her to marry him? She went pink, thinking about it, and felt all of a sudden wide awake and quite marvellous, which feeling prompted her to ask ill-advisedly:

'Why didn't you marry Susan? I should like to know about her—and you...' she paused, 'you said, just now, that you wanted to go to Paris to see her...'

She looked at him and saw that he wasn't only

annoyed; he was disconcerted as well. All the same, he said mildly, 'Yes, but I prefer not to discuss it.' He smiled very kindly at her, the sort of smile one gave when one was administering a snub to someone one didn't want to upset. Well, she had deserved it, she supposed. She said stiffly, 'What a delightful little garden this is,' and felt the colour wash her pale cheeks at his amused look. It was a relief when tea, borne out upon a vast silver tray and accompanied by a quantity of little cakes and sandwiches, proved a welcome diversion. She poured out carefully, and sampled the sandwiches, discovering that she had an appetite whatever her feelings, and after a few minutes she came to the conclusion that perhaps she had been unduly sensitive, for Constantijn went on talking without the merest hint of awkwardness. 'Yes, it's charming,' he agreed. 'I couldn't think of anywhere else as nice and as close to St Jude's.'

'Lady Belway wouldn't mind us coming?'

'Lord, no. Anyway, I asked Susan to tell her when I telephoned her earlier—this isn't the first time I've used her garden for a tea party.' He went on deliberately, 'You see, Augusta, how I am uncovering my—er—wicked past, but as I'm quite sure you wouldn't admit to loving me until I do... Am I not right?'

Augusta swallowed a morsel of cake without tasting any of it. 'Yes,' she said baldly. 'Did Susan mind? Me being here?'

She wasn't quite sure of the expression of his face. He said coolly enough, 'My dear good girl, how you do harp on Susan! I can't think why.' He put down his cup and got out of his chair to sit beside her. He took her cup too and put it on the table. 'And now,' he said blandly, 'if you feel like a nap?' She felt his arm around her shoulders; his own broad shoulder was invitingly near; she rested her head against it and said worriedly, 'We don't always agree, do we? And I'm never sure what you're thinking.'

'That's easily answered; two people who agree all the time would be so deadly dull they would destroy each other. And as to what I'm thinking—we'll leave that for the moment.' He went on more briskly, 'You had a pretty awful night, I imagine.'

'Grotty,' said Augusta pithily. 'All those poor people—more than fifty hurt, did you know? and twenty-three dead; I can't forget it.'

'Oh, yes, you can, Augusta. At least you can be thankful that you could do something to help them instead of just reading about them in the papers and wishing you could help.'

She nodded into his waistcoat. After a minute she asked, 'Do you know everyone at St Jude's?' and felt his chest heave with quiet laughter.

'Not everyone, but Dr Soames knows Rogers and Weller-Pratt, and remember, I'm his godson; I've known them since I was a small boy—just as I've known the Brigadier.'

She digested this and then asked a little shyly, 'And your mother?'

'She died a long time ago, when I was sixteen. Huib and I had grandparents in Holland and of course Lady Belway and Dr Soames over here. My father was broken-hearted when my mother died; we had never been very close, I suppose. He did everything to see that we had a good education and we lacked for nothing—only his affection. When I have children...' He paused and Augusta reached up quickly, kissed him fiercely and said in a warm voice, 'You'll be a wonderful father, and they'll all adore you because you'll love them so.'

He looked down at her, his eyes very bright. 'Yes, I believe I shall. Why did you kiss me?'

She stared back at him. 'Because I love you with all my heart and it hurts me to know that you could ever be unhappy.' She spoke with a little rush, made reckless by lack of sleep and nerves that were still tense. She hadn't meant to say it, but somehow she hadn't been able to stop herself. She looked away from him, feeling foolish and shy, and saw Sims coming out of the house towards them. She would have sat up, but Constantijn's hand on her shoulder held her firmly where she was while the old man delivered his message. 'There's a telephone call for you, sir, from Miss Susan, she says it's very urgent.'

Augusta felt Constantijn's arm slacken and withdraw. He said merely, 'I shan't be long.' She watched him stride away and there was no denying the urgency of his walk. She frowned a little; whatever Constantijn said, Susan seemed to loom very largely in his life...she was roused from thoughts which weren't happy by Sims' quiet voice asking if he should take away the tea things. He talked a little as he gathered them together; mild aimless remarks to which she replied just as aimlessly, but they had the effect of making everything normal again, so that when Constantijn returned after five minutes or so she was able to say in an ordinary, friendly voice, 'What a dear old man Sims is—has he been here long?'

He sat down, but this time in a chair. He looked pre-occupied, even vexed, but answered placidly enough, 'Oh, years—I remember him when I came here as a small boy with my parents. What would you like to do, Augusta? A drive into the country, perhaps, and dinner somewhere quiet?' She was about to agree to this reassuring suggestion when Sims appeared again. 'A call from Uldale, sir—for you.'

Constantijn got to his feet again; there was a little frown between his eyes, although he said casually enough, 'Forgive me, Augusta, but it may be important—there is something I must attend to.' He smiled at her. 'Why not have a nap while I'm gone?'

She had never felt further from napping. It was quite obvious that something was occupying his mind; it was equally obvious that he had no intention of telling her about it. When he came back, and this time it was ten minutes, and sat down again, his face was calm enough, but his pale eyes were hooded as he repeated his question just as though they had never been interrupted, but this time she had no intention of accepting; she said instead, 'Do you mind awfully if I go back to St Jude's? I really am tired.' She smiled and felt her heart lurch and drop at the relief, quickly concealed, which showed briefly in his eyes. All the same, he looked at his watch and said, 'I mind very much, but I'm not going to keep you out of your bed. By the way, this was propped up on the telephone table for you—for the post, I expect, but I see no reason why you shouldn't have it now.'

He dug a hand into a pocket and took out an envelope addressed to her in Lady Belway's copperplate handwriting. It was an invitation to Miss Susan Belsize's twenty-first birthday dance in ten days' time, and the old lady had written on the back, 'You must come, Augusta. If you have any difficulty in getting the evening off, let me know and I will arrange something. Susan will be disappointed if you refuse, and so shall I.'

Augusta looked up from reading it and found Constantijn's eyes upon her. He said, 'You'll come, of course.' She hesitated—there was no reason why she shouldn't accept, so she said slowly, 'Yes, I think I can get the evening off, unless Sister already has any plans for herself.' She studied the invitation card, not thinking of the dance at all but of Constantijn, who only a few days ago had told her that he was more than a little in love with her and that he was ready to wait—for her to make up her mind to marry him, presumably. Now, somehow, she wasn't sure if he had meant that at all. Perhaps he was in love with Susan and hoped to make her jealous. She looked up and found him looking at her.

He said, half laughing, 'Augusta, I believe you're weaving your tangled plots again.' He got up and came to sit beside her again. 'And not half an hour ago you told me that you loved me.' His voice was very gentle. 'If I asked you to marry me, would you say yes, I wonder? I had thought that this evening—but not now.' He turned her round to face him and she saw that he wasn't smiling. 'But when I do...you do love me, Roly?'

She answered quite crossly, for she was tired and doubtful and almost ready to burst into tears, 'Yes, I do, and I can't think why,' and was at once swept close and kissed as gently as he had spoken. Presently he said, 'Don't mind if you don't see or hear from me for a few days; I have to go up to Cumberland—I'll let you know when I get back.'

Augusta, her head snugly against his shoulder again, thought sleepily that Uldale was in Cumbria—

what could there be there that was so important? Her mind refused to grapple with the problem; she was lulled into a feeling of security by his calm nearness, and sat quietly without speaking until with an effort she roused herself. 'I shall be asleep in a minute. I'd better go, or you'll have to carry me like poor little Meek.'

He took her to the door of the Nurses' Home and under Valky's delighted gaze, kissed her again.

'When are you going to Cumbria?' asked Augusta sleepily. 'Not tonight?'

'Probably—it depends on a number of things. I must telephone Paris first. Don't worry your head about it now.' He kissed her again lightly and she went inside and up to her room and got ready for bed, wanting to think about why he needed to telephone Paris but too tired to do so. She got into bed and was asleep as her head touched the pillow.

CHAPTER EIGHT

SHE SAW HIM the very next day, for her services had been borrowed by the Accident Room to escort a man with a fractured spine to Stoke Mandeville. They were approaching the A40 when the ambulance they were in was held up in a traffic block and the Rolls with Constantijn driving, slid to a halt beside them. It was so close that she could have opened the window and touched the car with her hand, instead she sat staring at him and at Susan sitting beside him. They were talking—arguing—she thought, and once he turned away and stared up at the darkened windows of the ambulance, and although she knew that he couldn't see her she drew back instinctively. He looked tired and angry and worried, and Susan had been crying. The ambulance moved on as the traffic ahead sorted itself out, and presently when the road was clear the Rolls shot past them and disappeared within seconds.

It was only much later, when she had returned to St Jude's, that she was able to think about it, for she had had the patient to look after and on the return journey she had sat in front with the ambulance men, and they had talked cheerfully and without pause all the way back. But now in her room, still in uniform, she tried to sort out her thoughts. Constantijn had told her that he was going to Cumbria but that he would telephone Paris first—to Susan, no doubt—and she

180

had come back; probably she was going to Cumbria with him, Augusta wasn't sure, but it seemed likely that the A40 joined up with the M6 somewhere or other. She was a little hazy about that part of the country, but she was almost sure that that was so.

But why had Constantijn looked so angry and why had Susan been in tears, and above all, why hadn't he told her at least something of the truth? Surely, she thought drearily, if a man loved a girl, even only a little, he trusted her too? Perhaps he didn't love her... She cried about this for quite some minutes, then resolutely washed her face and did her hair and sat down to think again, this time about Lady Belway—why had it been so necessary for her to go to Paris just to see Susan?—no light undertaking with a wheelchair and the nurse and sticks to walk with; and was it because of her visit that Susan was back in England, or because of something Constantijn had said to her?

Augusta gave up at last, for she was unable to think of any more answers. She lay in bed remembering how she had told Constantijn that she loved him, and wished with all her being that she hadn't. She turned and twisted, trying to get away from the memory of it, and at last went to sleep.

She felt better in the morning, for common sense told her that there must be some logical explanation for it all, and all she had to do was to wait until she saw Constantijn again. She posted her acceptance of Lady Belway's invitation and was so determinedly bright and cheerful that her friends became a little puzzled; not that she wasn't bright and cheerful by nature, but this was something different and almost painful in its persistence. But the cheerfulness wore a little thin after four days had gone by, during which time she hadn't heard a word from Constantijn. He had told her she wouldn't hear from him, but that made it no easier. She entered, rather half-heartedly, into the various discussions as to what she should wear to the dance and was at length persuaded to buy a new dress—a dream in aubergine pleated chiffon. She bought sandals too with pearl tassels on the insteps, and held a dress rehearsal that evening, and Wilkes, who was rather good with hair, made a complicated pile of curls on top of her head, while several friends offered a variety of evening wraps. Augusta thought that they were probably enjoying it all far more than she was.

It was the following day over a hurried breakfast that Bates mentioned that she had seen Susan Belsize the previous day. 'Coming out of Cartier's, my dears, and very dishy too. She had that tall fair man with her—the one who used to come and see Lady Belway when I was on PP. Very wrapped up in each other they were too.' She glanced down the table to where Augusta was sitting. 'He dangled after you a bit, didn't he, Gussie? Well, my dear, you've got some stiff opposition there.'

Everyone laughed and Augusta laughed with them because no one knew how she felt about Constantijn and it was only a joke, but like so many jokes, it had a sting in its tail, because even if he had dangled after her it hadn't come to much. She got up with the others

and went along to the ward to start the day's work—
there was nothing like work to stop one thinking.

Everything went wrong from the start—it was one
of those mornings when charts got mislaid, X-rays
which should have been there weren't and a precious
specimen for the path. lab. was thrown away by an
overzealous nurse, and Mr Rogers, when he did his
round, found fault with everything. When he had
gone, Augusta went with Sister to the office and
poured the coffee which they drank in a gloomy silence, but presently Sister said more cheerfully,
'Thank God for my weekend—which reminds me, I
quite forgot to ask you—I don't suppose you feel like
adding a half day to your days off and coming back
at one on Saturday? You've some time due to you
from that night's work you put in—you could go after
second dinner. Only Reg'—Reg was her boy-friend—
'is coming down for the weekend…'

Augusta agreed at once. She would go home, even
for so short a time and forget all about Constantijn.
'If I could just fly over and telephone home so someone can meet me?' she asked.

'Of course—you're sure you don't mind? It's such
short notice, but you're off next weekend, aren't
you?' Augusta nodded, not really minding very much.
What was the use of being off duty if Constantijn was
miles away and didn't care anyway? She thought she
probably wouldn't go to the wretched dance at all.
She resolutely tore her thoughts away and attended
carefully to Sister's instructions for the morning and
presently followed her back to the ward, telling herself how lucky she was to have an unexpected day at

home and ignoring the small voice at the back of her head demanding to know what would happen if Constantijn called and she wasn't in the hospital. 'Serve him right,' she muttered as she scrubbed up to do dressings.

Her mother met her at Sherborne and Augusta drove the Morris home, while she told, at some length, of the happenings of the last few days. She took pains to recount everything in great detail, although she touched so lightly on Constantijn's visit to the ward and their tea together that anyone listening might have deduced that the occasions were of such minor importance that they had all but slipped her memory. But her mother, who wasn't just anyone, drew her own conclusions. When Augusta at length came to the end of her story, she said:

'How very exciting, Roly darling. Are you going to marry Constantijn?'

Taken off her guard, Augusta changed gear with an appalling grinding sound and sent the elderly car thundering round a curve. Only then did she decide to answer her mother's question.

She said slowly and rather inadequately, 'He hasn't asked me—I mean not so that I can say yes or no.'

'But you'll say yes?'

She nodded. 'Well, I let him see...but something's holding him back. Oh, I know I've been cross and tired and it must have put him off—but it's more than that.'

'You don't want to talk about it?'

'No, Mother dear, I don't—you understand, don't you?' She went on, with determined brightness,

'How's everyone? I had a long letter from Tante Emma—have you heard too?'

The talk settled down to a casual exchange of everyday family happenings until Augusta turned the car in through the gate and pulled up before the open door.

The house stood, warm and quiet in the afternoon sunlight, surrounded by its lovely, rather untidy garden. The dogs came bounding to meet them followed by Maudie and Fred, and they all trooped into the house together. Augusta went up to her room, with Fred, who had a loving nature, draped over one shoulder, and thought how nice it was to be home with time to think quietly.

But by mid-morning the following day, she had done no thinking at all. The afternoon and evening had gone like a flash, and contrary to her expectations, she had slept all night. She worked away at Bottom's plump sides, putting a gloss on to his coat and singing odds and ends of tunes under her breath. When Bottom turned his head at the sound of footsteps she stopped her singing to look as well and saw Constantijn making his way in a leisurely manner towards them. When he was near enough, he said, 'Hullo, my darling Miss Brown—how is it you're not lying back in a hammock in your yellow dress, dreaming of me?'

Augusta waited a minute to allow her breath to become normal.

'If I'd known that you were coming,' she began, 'I would have done just that.' She sounded a little cross, as indeed she was, aware that slacks and a cotton sweater of a much washed blue did very little for her appearance, and aware too that the sight of him had tumbled all her doubts and muddled thought out of her mind and that all that mattered was that he had come and she was overjoyed to see him again.

He came close and when Bottom lifted an ear invitingly, obliged the beast by scratching it gently while he studied Augusta. He said after a pause, 'You'll do very well as you are,' and leaned forward over Bottom's furry head and kissed her cheek. 'If you don't mind going back to St Jude's this evening instead of tomorrow morning, I'll drive you up—we could have a meal on the way.'

Augusta stroked the donkey's soft nose and said rather uncertainly, 'Oh, are you going back to London again?'

'Yes, until after Susan's dance.' His voice had been light and he had smiled, but all the same she had the impression that any questions she might ask would be ignored or at least circumvented. She said:

'All right. Thank you very much,' and knew that her words were trite; she wished that her voice didn't sound so stiff and unfriendly despite her feelings, and when he said gently, 'I thought you would be pleased to see me,' she changed colour slightly, longing to ask a dozen questions of him although common sense told her that it would be unwise to do so. She allowed common sense to take over. 'I'm very pleased to see you,' she said. 'You took me by surprise,' and smiled at him. He stared back at her, half-smiling himself. 'That's better,' he said, and abandoned Bottom's ear, picked up the curry-comb from the wall and took her arm.

'Are you going to invite me to lunch?'

Augusta, feeling the touch of his hand on her arm, would have invited him to anything at that moment. 'Yes, of course—only isn't Doctor Soames expecting you?'

He shook his head. 'I didn't get back to town until very late last night and I came straight here from St Jude's.'

Augusta gave him a questioning look and he went on in a comfortably ordinary voice, 'I went there to see when you were off duty. I tried to get back in time to see you last night, but I got held up and I couldn't very well have broken into the Nurses' Home at two o'clock in the morning. As it was you weren't there anyway.'

They started to saunter across the paddock towards the house. 'Tell me what you've been doing with yourself, my dear girl.'

It was the very question she would have liked to put to him herself, but he had, after all, come hotfoot down to Dorset. 'Oh, very dull,' she said, to be interrupted blandly with his 'Well, yes—naturally. I wasn't there, was I?'

It seemed the conversation was to be kept light, so she laughed. 'Yes—if you need your ego boosted, which I doubt. Actually it wasn't all that dull. I bought a new dress for Lady Belway's party, and borrowed a cloak from one of the girls and practised a new way of doing my hair.'

He stopped. 'How are you going to do it?'

'Not me—I'm incapable of doing more than screwing it up on top—one of the girls is super at doing hair.'

She took a step forward, but he held her with a detaining hand. 'Dearest Miss Brown,' he said, 'will you—just for me—leave your rusty locks as they are? I like them that way.'

Augusta looked astonished. 'Just any old how?' she inquired.

He laughed. 'Well, put a few extra curls in if it will make you happy.'

He was staring at her again; his eyes, which she had always thought so strangely light, looked dark and deep. She said, a little breathless, 'If—if you want me to. It doesn't really matter—it won't make any difference to my face, you know.'

Constantijn pulled her close without haste. He said seriously, 'No, nothing could make any difference to your face—or to you.' He smiled suddenly and his eyes lost their strange darkness. 'What is this dress like?' his voice was light, almost teasing.

Augusta replied promptly, 'Oh, gorgeous. A Jean Allen model—pleated chiffon in aubergine. It makes my hair less carroty.'

'That's a pity, for I find that carroty hair is my favourite colour after all.'

She stared up at him. 'You said you didn't like it,' she stated flatly and then, catching the twinkle in his eyes, went on hurriedly, 'Come on, we shall be late for lunch and I promised I'd lay the table.' She looked down at her person. 'And now I'll have to change too.'

'For me? Why? I'm not a stranger, am I? At least, I hope not.'

They had walked on as they talked, now he stopped again and deliberately pulled her to him, and uncaring of her mother's interested gaze from the kitchen door, kissed her with slow pleasure.

Luncheon was a gay meal with a great deal of laughter and talk and not so much as a raised eyebrow when Constantijn referred to her as his darling Miss Brown, but presently he went away, saying that he had to see his godfather and had several important telephone calls to make besides, and as he said it Augusta watched the furrow of worry come and go between his brows and then forgot about it when he said he would be back after tea to pick her up. He smiled at her as he said it so that her heart turned over.

He had mentioned a meal on the way—it seemed an excellent chance to wear the yellow dress, especially as he remembered it. She packed her few things directly he had gone, laid the dress ready on the bed, and went into the garden to do some quite unnecessary work. She had been poking around with her trowel for half an hour or so when her mother, who had been lying with her feet up in the hammock, opened her eyes. Augusta cast down the trowel and said without preamble, 'Mother, there is something, isn't there?'

Mrs Brown had no difficulty in interpreting this statement. 'Dear Roly, yes, I think there is—but forgo my egg money if it's anything he's ashamed of.' Her daughter heaved a sigh of relief. Mrs Brown's egg money was, though not exactly riches, a nice little sum, largely due to the fact that she had long ago persuaded her husband that he should pay for the hens' feed, and for the boy who cleaned out the hen-house, thus leaving her a splendid profit—it was a token of her faith in Constantijn that she should even suggest giving up this handsome addition to her allowance. She arranged herself comfortably in the hammock and went on in a soothing voice. 'Your father likes him, Roly. Could you not stop worrying about whatever it is that's worrying you, darling? You're so obviously...' She stopped and started again. 'Enjoy your evening—I should think he's great fun to be with.'

Augusta had abandoned her gardening and was sitting on the grass. 'Yes, he is. I forget everything else when I'm with him.' She eyed her mother a little defiantly, wondering if that lady would smile because it had sounded a bit corny, but Mrs Brown replied quite seriously, 'Yes, dear...it's nice, isn't it, and it stays that way—provided you marry the right man.'

'Like Father?' asked Augusta.

'Like your father,' said Mrs Brown, and smiled. She watched Augusta fidgeting on the grass and said with maternal cunning, 'Darling, be an angel and make some scones for tea, I'm quite exhausted in this heat.' She lay back, looking fragile as her daughter obediently got to her feet. There was plenty for tea without scones, but the dear child would find the afternoon pass more quickly if she had something to do.

Augusta was dressed and ready by the time Constantijn arrived. He was late, but he excused himself with such charm that it was difficult to be annoyed, especially when his eyes told her that she had done the right thing in wearing the yellow dress.

They waved their cheerful farewells, and he turned the car into one of the several small side roads which led, each in its own roundabout fashion, to the A30 and London. Once on it, he gave the Rolls her head, for there was surprisingly little traffic about for a Friday evening. Augusta, watching the country whizz past, felt a vague disappointment; at the rate they were travelling they would be at their journey's end in two or three hours, and he hadn't mentioned food...indeed, the conversation was of a most impersonal nature, although when she led the talk to Alkmaar and her aunts, he was ready enough to respond. All the same, something was worrying him; she could tell because of the tiny furrow between his sandy brows. They slowed through Shaftesbury and then sped on towards Salisbury, and he said, so suddenly that she jumped:

'It must seem to you, my dear Roly, that I'm intent on getting you back to St Jude's as fast as possible. Well, I'm not. There's a small village near Guildford—Compton; I've booked a table at Withies, which is a restaurant I've been to before. I think you'll like it, and it's well under an hour's run to town, so we need not hurry over dinner. You can go in as late as you like?'

She said happily, 'Oh, yes—and I'm not on until one.'

'I thought of that.' He gave her a brief, smiling sidelong glance. 'How pretty you look in that yellow thing. You're so composed, Augusta, not for ever asking questions and wanting things and having hysterics when you can't get them.' Which remark caused her to say quickly, 'But I never have hysterics,' and made her wonder if he was thinking of Susan, but how could she ask that after what he had just said? She inquired after Johanna instead, which led the conversation naturally enough to Paris where she now was and which Augusta knew of a little as she had been there several times. They exchanged views and opinions and argued with a pleasure which they both enjoyed until they had almost reached Guildford, when Constantijn turned off on to a side road and presently parked the car outside Withies. It was a smallish restaurant, but the food was excellent. They chose from a cold table of great variety and Constantijn ordered a bottle of champagne, which surprised her until he said, the moment the waiter had left them, 'You must know what I'm going to say, my dearest Augusta. Will you marry me?'

She restrained herself from shouting Yes at the top of her voice and instead looked across the table at him with commendable calm. The furrow had gone, she noticed, perhaps he had been plucking up courage...she dismissed the thought at once; Constantijn wasn't a man who needed to pluck up courage, but whatever it was, it had gone from his face, leaving no trace. She said quietly, 'Yes, Constantijn, I will,' and smiled, at the same time concealing her disappointment—a half-full restaurant wouldn't have been her choice—but then it wasn't for a girl to choose.

As though he had read her thoughts: 'I wanted to ask you this morning,' he said, 'but your mother...'

Augusta chuckled. 'Don't tell me you're afraid of her!'

'No—she's a delightful person, but I somehow felt that privacy at such a moment...and I never have fancied proposing while driving a car at speed, and anticipating the remainder of the evening, I couldn't quite bring myself to ask you in St Jude's entrance hall with, very possibly, the hall porter making an interested third. It had to be here.'

She had to laugh at that. They drank champagne then, and ate their meal in such a leisurely manner that it was, incredibly, well after eleven when they left. In the car he kissed her, and said:

'Once this dance is over, we'll make wedding plans, shall we?'

Augusta was still a little dizzy from his kiss, and said in a voice that wasn't quite steady, 'Yes, if you like. I expect you've an awful lot to do.'

He nodded. 'Quite a bit, although I shall be handing over Susan's affairs as soon as my guardianship ends.'

She was unable to prevent herself from asking, 'I expect you will give her a splendid present?' To which he made no answer, merely saying, 'Which reminds me—have you any preference as to your ring, Augusta?'

'Me? I don't know—I haven't had time. I think I'd like to be surprised.'

'Surprised you shall be, Roly dear.' He took his

hand off the wheel and touched hers for a fleeting second.

They reached St Jude's after midnight and the night porter gave them a sleepy glance as they went past his little box. They didn't hurry and Augusta was glad because the idea of parting from Constantijn, even for a short time, was unbearable…when they reached the door at the end of the passage he opened it and then stood leaning against the wall watching her; she said in a little rush, 'Thank you for bringing me back and for giving me dinner,' although what she really wanted to say was 'I love you', but somehow she was unable to say it, and anyway, it didn't matter, for he took her in his arms and said softly, 'How sweet you are—and I'm the one who should give thanks,' and kissed her again so that presently she floated across the courtyard and up the stairs to her room, where she undressed without being aware of doing so and got into bed, to lie thinking happily of the future.

There were flowers from him next day, but no message. She had expected a telephone call or perhaps a letter, and when neither came she consoled herself with the fact that he had said that he was going to be busy. The next day was Sunday, so there was no post anyway and probably he was back with Doctor Soames. She could hardly eat her breakfast on Monday, wondering if there would be a letter, and she had to wait two or three hours before she knew, as it was theatre day and she went down with the first case and stayed to help the anaesthetist. There was a letter, or rather a note, written in a laconic style which held no trace of a love letter; it merely told her that he would call for her the following evening at nine o'clock, and was signed, Yours, C. She read it several times; even if he was hers. C. he didn't sound wildly enthusiastic about it—perhaps he wasn't the kind of man who could put his feelings into writing; she thought soberly that she had a great deal to learn about him.

She was ready the following evening long before nine o'clock. Several of her friends had given her assistance of a sort—it took the form of sitting on her bed, drinking tea and commenting upon each stage of her toilet, allied with a good deal of speculative talk about the evening before her. It was Wilkes who offered to go downstairs and see if Constantijn had arrived. She came tearing back almost at once. 'He's here, Gussie—he's in tails and he looks marvellous!'

Augusta sprayed Balmain's Jolie Madame with a careful hand. She said, 'Yes—I thought he would be,' and when Wilkes asked, 'I say, he sent the roses, didn't he?' she said 'Yes,' again. She put down the scent spray, flung her borrowed cape around her shoulders and went to the door.

'Don't drink all the tea,' she said, and then, as a kind of afterthought, 'I'm going to marry him.'

She could hear their excited burst of talk as she went down the stairs to where Constantijn stood waiting for her. She put up her face to be kissed much as a child would and felt his lips gentle on her cheek.

'You smell nice, Roly, and how beautifully punctual. Am I allowed to see your dress, or must I wait?'

She slid off the cloak promptly, glad that he had asked, and stood quietly under his gaze. 'Yes—it's perfect,' he said. 'You'll certainly get your share of admiring glances, my dear. You're positively beautiful.'

She said without selfconsciousness, 'That's because I'm in love,' and smiled at him. He caught her hand in both of his, staring down at her.

'I told you you were sweet,' he said, 'I can only say it again,' and he bent and kissed her again, on her mouth, and not gently at all.

The dance was well under way when they arrived, although there were still other guests going in as they went into the house. The hall looked very splendid and brilliantly lighted, and Augusta felt a small twinge of panic as they entered it, to be at once soothed by Constantijn's calm voice saying mildly, 'I'll be here when you're ready, Roly,' as he handed her over to a maid she had already met when she had lunched with Lady Belway.

They went upstairs slowly, his hand on her elbow, and across a wide landing to the ballroom at the back of the house. It was a fair size and very full of people. Lady Belway was sitting just inside the door, greeting her guests, with Susan standing beside her, looking beautiful in a dress of silver tissue which had doubtless cost a fortune. Augusta offered a polite hand to the old lady and was pulled down to receive a peck upon her cheek and a warm greeting, while Susan added, 'I'm so glad you could make it, Augusta.' But though she smiled as she spoke there was a lack of warmth about her which Augusta was quick to notice, and she couldn't help hearing her 'I must see you, Constantijn,' as he stopped to talk to her. Augusta, with Constantijn's hand on her arm, moved down the room, telling herself that naturally Susan would want to see Constantijn—he was, after all, for a few more hours at least, still her guardian—but why had she sounded so desperately urgent? She pushed the thought to one side and gave all her attention to the various people she was being introduced to, and presently, when Constantijn said, 'If we don't dance now, we may not get the chance for a little while,' she forgot everything.

They danced until the music finally stopped and Huib, appearing silently beside them, declared that it was his turn and whirled her away so that in a moment she had lost sight of Constantijn. After that she danced with a bewildering succession of partners, so that it was considerably more than a little while before he claimed her once more, and they had barely taken a dozen steps when an imposing figure tapped Constantijn on one shoulder and when they came to a halt, said in a rich, heavily accented voice, 'My dear boy, I have been waiting to dance all the evening with this young lady—may I be allowed to claim that privilege now, before I must so regrettably leave? You do not mind?'

He smiled with great charm upon them both and Constantijn said, 'I mind very much, Your Excellency, but I hate to see you disappointed, and I'm sure Miss Brown feels the same,' and in no time at all, Augusta found herself with her new partner. He was elderly and portly and grey-bearded and wore a magnificent uniform which she completely failed to recognise. Constantijn had introduced him, certainly, but the name had sounded outlandish and she wasn't

quite sure from which part of the world he came—
apparently it didn't matter, for he talked very little
and then only banalities, but he danced with an ex-
pertise which, though old-fashioned, was a nice
change from some of her partners of the evening, who
had tended either to shuffle round and round or go in
for a great deal of hip-shaking and wriggling—not
Constantijn, of course, who danced with a kind of
careless perfection which most happily matched her
own. It was while she was gyrating upon the dance
floor with this interesting personage that she caught
Lady Belway's eye, and obedient to its imperious
summons, went to her side.

'I'm feeling cold,' said the old lady a little grumpily, 'and I can see nobody—nobody at all to do the
smallest service for me. Be a good child and go to
my room and bring me back my shawl you will find
on the chair by the window—Paisley—my dear
mother's, and a very fine one too.'

Augusta gave her partner an apologetic glance and
said, 'Yes, of course I'll fetch it for you, Lady Belway…if you will tell me where your room is?'

'It is on this floor—take the left-hand fork at the
top of the stairs as you leave this room—it is the last
door at the end of the corridor.'

Augusta made her way slowly through the crowded
room, looking about her for Constantijn as she went,
for despite the crush he was easy enough to see by
reason of his height. There was no sign of him, however, and she frowned a little, suppressing a not un-
natural annoyance; she had enough good sense not to
expect him to follow her around like her own shadow,

but even so, surely he could have waited until His Excellency Someone-or-other was ready to hand her back again? She opened the door of Lady Belway's room and went inside. It was a large apartment with equally large french windows opening on to a balcony, and as the curtains had not been drawn it was not necessary to put on the light—she could see the chair by the window and the shawl upon it. She crossed the room to pick it up and paused for a moment to stand and look out upon the garden below where she and Constantijn had had tea. It was then that she became aware of his voice, so close that she looked round, startled, half expecting to see him in the room. Certainly she heard every word as clearly as though he were.

'Susan, it's impossible,' he was saying, 'I thought we had decided that only this morning.' He sounded patient and at the same time exasperated, but Susan, when she answered, sounded tearful.

'Why not? You've changed so, Constantijn. You always said you wanted me to be happy, and now you don't care any more.'

'You wouldn't be happy at someone else's expense, can't you see that? What has she ever done to you that you should blight her whole life? She's sweet and kind and trusting, and she's in love.'

'I don't care a damn for her—and I'm in love too, or had you forgotten that?'

His voice sounded weary. 'No—I haven't been allowed to, have I? But I gave my word to her and I don't intend to go back on it, and when I see her,' he paused, 'believe me, Susan, if I can find a way out of this mess, it won't be at her expense.'

Augusta stood very still, aware of an unpleasant coldness deep inside her. They were, of course, talking about her, who else? She remembered with horrid clarity that she had told Constantijn that she loved him, and now that she came to think about it he had never once said that he loved her. A kind of numbing emptiness took possession of her which did not allow of her thinking and which held at bay any other feelings. She picked up the shawl, and folding it carefully, draped it over one arm and waited with a frozen calm for the conversation to continue, intent on hearing everything. But there wasn't a great deal more to hear. Susan's voice, resentful and angry, 'When are you getting married?' and she heard Constantijn reply, 'My dear Susan, surely you realise that this thing must be settled first?' and then more briskly, 'Dry your eyes and do something to your face—everyone will wonder where you have got to, and I'll have no suspicion of gossip. Pin a smile on your face and come and cut the cake.'

Augusta moved at last; she would have to get back to the ballroom before they did. If Constantijn should notice her returning after them, he was astute enough to wonder where she had been, and of one thing she was quite certain, she must do and say nothing which might give him cause to wonder. Later, when her wits were working again, she would think what to do, although she was already miserably aware that she already knew. She went back to the ballroom, arranged the shawl around Lady Belway's shoulders and was dancing with a suave gentleman with a peculiar accent and a great many medals on his chest, when she saw Susan and Constantijn return. Susan was whisked away to dance at once, but Constantijn remained by the door, looking around him.

Augusta, steeling herself, smiled gaily when he saw her and waved a hand airily, and only when there was the length of the room between them did she suggest to her partner that some sort of refreshment would be nice. This strategic move had the effect of keeping her away from the dance floor for at least a quarter of an hour, and by that time Susan was ready to cut the gigantic cake which had been carried in, and even then she was able to put off talking to Constantijn, for he had a speech to make and stood, naturally enough, with Susan and Lady Belway and the rest of the family. It was fortunate that her partner seemed loath to part with her anyway, which was perhaps a good thing, she reflected, especially as he set about introducing several of his friends to her as well and she found herself hedged in by would-be partners.

The cake was cut, the champagne drunk and the speeches made, and it was only when Constantijn was making his speech that the numbness gave way to pain and bewilderment that he should ever have thought himself sufficiently in love with her to ask her to marry him. But perhaps he had never meant it to go so far—perhaps he had wanted to make Susan jealous, perhaps even, he had only discovered his true feelings for Susan in his imagined love for herself. He had said once that he had thought of marrying

Susan. If only she had never told him that she loved him...

She allowed herself to be led on to the dance floor again and turned a bright, attentive face to her partner while she went on thinking about Constantijn. Well, now he could marry his Susan, and she would tell him so just as soon as the opportunity occurred. She had a weekend, she reflected, just four days away. He had said that he would be with Dr Soames for a day or so before he went back to Alkmaar; she would go down and see him and arrange everything in the friendliest possible fashion; she would have to think exactly what she must say, but there was plenty of time for that. Augusta felt almost lighthearted with relief at her decision and the smile she directed at her partner was almost dazzling.

Constantijn claimed her a few minutes later, cutting in with smooth good manners which left her partner with nothing to say. He said in her ear, 'Having a good time, Roly?'

'Oh, marvellous.' She shot him a quick glance, taking care to be very natural. Rather pleased with her efforts, she went on gaily, 'You made a super speech,' and heard him say over her head, 'Yes—what's the matter, Augusta?'

It was so unexpected that she was unable to say anything for a moment. To deny it altogether would be of no use. She said carefully, 'Nothing really. It's just that I've met so many people and I'm not used to this sort of thing—I think I feel a little overwhelmed.' She addressed his white shirt front, for to look at him was beyond her. 'Susan looked gorgeous, didn't she? How long does the junketing last?'

He disposed of this conversational gambit with a brief, 'Yes, she did,' and, 'Breakfast at five o'clock. When are you free tomorrow?'

She was able to answer with perfect truth. 'I'm not—at least, I've got an on at one, and I must get some sleep first.'

'The evening?'

'I shan't be off until nine o'clock, and you know what that means by the time the report's given.'

'Any weekends in the offing?'

The lie came with surprising ease. 'Afraid not—I swopped with Sister.' Not for the world would she tell him that she was free the following weekend. She had to have time to think what she was going to say, and until she was ready to say it, the less she saw of him the better.

'When are you going back to Holland?' she asked.

'Not until Monday—which means that I shan't see you before I go. I'll telephone you; there must be some corner of time we can snatch before then.'

'All right.' Before she could say any more, he went on silkily, 'You know, if it were anyone else but you, dear Augusta, I should think you were playing hard to get.'

She addressed his shirt front once more, keeping her voice cheerfully matter-of-fact. 'Well, I'm not anyone else, and you know how difficult it is to plan a social life when you're a nurse.' She risked a quick look at him; he was smiling a little, completely at ease and not, she concluded crossly, particularly upset at the idea of not seeing her. She asked gaily, 'Who was the man I was dancing with—the one with all the medals?' and he seemed quite content to allow the conversation to drift away into small talk until presently they parted again. It was almost three o'clock when he swung her on to the floor again and this time she asked, 'Would you mind very much if I went back to St Jude's soon?'

'Never tired?' he queried lazily.

'A little—it was theatre day, you know—and yesterday too.'

He said at once, 'Dear Roly, what a thoughtless fool I am! I'll take you back now and you must promise me that you'll go to bed and not get up until you go on duty tomorrow.'

He took her arm and led her over to Lady Belway's chair and as they went she laughed a little. 'That's an easy promise to keep—easier than most,' and stopped because of what she had almost said, but he didn't appear to have heard her and driving her back to the hospital, he talked only of their evening, and that casually as though he were making himself agreeable to someone he was giving a lift home. At St Jude's she said quickly, 'Don't get out,' but could have saved her breath, for he went with her through the quiet entrance lobby and along the passage just as he had done before, only this time she was unhappy and then she had floated along in a wonderful dream. At the door he kissed her gently and said merely, 'Sleep well, dear Roly,' and although she was certain that he was going to say something else, he didn't, but waited by the door until she reached the door of the Nurses' Home and turned to wave to him.

CHAPTER NINE

SHE THOUGHT ABOUT him a great deal during the next few days. He had suggested telephoning, and when he didn't her disappointment was tempered with relief because she wanted to be quite sure of herself before she saw him again. He was probably already at Doctor Soames' and, she thought wryly, probably Susan was there as well. She hoped she wouldn't need to meet Susan, especially now that she knew what she had to say, although she was still a little uncertain as to how to say it. She was conscious of rage as well as unhappiness now, although she was determined to show nothing but a cool dignified front when she met Constantijn. But as the weekend approached, she became more and more edgy so that the nurses on the ward, accustomed to her calm good nature, stood aghast while she vented a spleen they didn't know she had.

Her mother was at Sherborne to meet her, and if she found her daughter silent on the journey home, she made no comment, but talked about everything under the sun excepting Constantijn. It was Augusta who mentioned him. 'Is he at Dr Soames', Mother?' she asked lightly. 'He's going back to Alkmaar on Monday, you know—we haven't been able to see each other for a little while.'

Mrs Brown, concealing with admirable aplomb the

205

fact that Constantijn had told her only the previous day that her daughter wasn't free that weekend, said that yes, she fancied he was still there for Dr Soames had gone down to Exeter to watch county cricket, and presumably someone was taking his surgery. She then plunged into a maze of questions concerning the dance which kept both ladies nicely occupied until they reached home. There Mrs Brown, with maternal cunning, suggested to Augusta that she might like to put the car away and then stroll down to the paddock to say hullo to Bottom, while she herself just popped in to see if supper was getting on. This manoeuvre gave her the necessary time to find her husband and son and warn them to be careful what they said to Roly because there was something wrong, although she didn't know what. 'And,' she went on, 'don't say anything about Lady Belway being down here or that she's coming to tea tomorrow,' and when they wanted to know why merely stated maddeningly that she didn't know but they would probably find out before it was too late.

They all three turned to stare out of the window at Augusta walking up from the paddock, not knowing that she was under observation; she looked dejected and unhappy, but as she neared the house she quickened her pace and lifted her head. Obviously, whatever it was, they were not going to be told about it.

She spent the next morning mooning around, practising her carefully thought out speech on Bottom, waiting for the afternoon. As it was Friday there was surgery from three to four as well as from six to seven. She had made up her mind to go just before four, see Constantijn as soon as the last patient had gone, and come home again. Beyond this point she didn't choose to think. Soon after three she went up to her room and changed into the mouse-coloured dress, did her hair with tremendous care, her face too, and went downstairs to find her mother in the garden and tell her with a false cheerfulness that she was taking the car for half an hour.

A few minutes later she turned the Morris's elderly nose towards the village, driving rather too fast because she knew the road so well and didn't care anyway. It was a pity that she had to slow down to keep pace with the local bus just ahead of her. It was lumbering along in its own good time, stopping every few hundred yards to put off and pick up its familiar passengers. There was a farm transporter behind her too, so that she had to pay attention to her driving, which accounted for her not seeing Lady Belway's Daimler, with Lady Belway in it, glide past in the opposite direction. In the village at last, she turned the car off the road into the doctor's short drive and got out to go in through the open surgery door at the side of the house, before she could change her mind. Miss Pink, who had been with Dr Soames for as long as Augusta could remember, lifted her alert, middle-aged face to look at her as she went in and said, 'Hullo, Gussie dear. Dr Soames is away.'

'Yes, I know,' said Augusta. 'I came to see Constantijn.' She looked round the empty waiting room. 'Is there anyone with him?'

'Yes, dear, old Mrs Trent—her legs, you know—

she won't be long now, though. Would you like me to tell Doctor you're here?'

Augusta answered a shade too quickly, 'No—oh, no, thank you, Pinky, I'll surprise him.'

But when she opened the door of the consulting room a few minutes later, he didn't look in the least surprised. Pleased, yes, and something else she couldn't define. Before she could speak he had got up from his chair and come to meet her. 'Hullo, Augusta. I rather expected you, although I believe you have come for all the wrong reasons—all the same, I'm enchanted to see you.' He spoke unhurriedly and with no sign of unease, but she caught a gleam in his eye quite at variance with his tone. 'Sit down, won't you?'

'No,' said Augusta, her voice a little too loud. 'I've made up my mind to talk to you about something and I'd like to say it and go.'

'About us?' he queried gently.

'Yes.' When she had rehearsed her speech during long wakeful nights and again into Bottom's woolly neck, it had seemed simple enough; now it was a different matter. She was silent so long that Constantijn asked blandly, 'Hard to start?—perhaps I could help?'

She looked at him then, standing in front of the desk, his hands in his pockets, rattling his loose change—they had laughed about that habit of his not so long ago. She swallowed the rage she could feel welling up inside her, glad that its very strength made it easier. She found her voice at last, still too loud but quite steady.

'At the dance the other night, Lady Belway sent me to fetch her shawl from her room. The window was open—I heard you and Susan talking. I should have gone away at once, I suppose, but you were talking about me, so I listened.' She wasn't looking at him any more, so she didn't see his lifted eyebrows but rushed on with her well-rehearsed recital. 'I shouldn't have done that, I'm sorry. I've been thinking about it ever since and I've quite made up my mind. I wouldn't marry you if you were the last man on earth.'

She had been speaking quite calmly, but now suddenly misery and temper took over from the sweet reasonableness she had practised so hard.

'How could you possibly expect me?' she asked snappily. 'I told you I hadn't got a weekend.'

'So you did—and it was such a palpable fib that I telephoned the hospital to find out for myself.'

Augusta choked. 'You didn't telephone me...'

'No. What would have been the point? You would have only had to think up more fibs.' She looked at him quickly; his voice had been placid, but she could see the corner of his mouth twitch—he was finding it amusing, no doubt. She said, her voice a little too high as well as too loud, 'You told me once that I was old-fashioned, and I think I must be—I...' She stopped because the tears in her throat were making it impossible to talk. Her green eyes flashed at him, standing there staring back at her with expressionless pale gaze. She mastered her childish desire to burst into tears and said fiercely, 'You're—you're...can't you say anything?' Her voice, despite her efforts, had risen again.

He answered her unhurriedly, 'No, I think not, dear Roly, not just at this minute, for you are beside yourself with rage, are you not? Perhaps later...'

'I won't be here later,' said Augusta between her teeth, 'and how dare you call me Roly! Only my—my nearest and dearest call me that.'

'And I am neither?' he queried silkily. 'What are you going to do now?'

'I'm going home.' She swept past him, her strange carroty hair a-glow with rage, her eyes sparkling. She looked, in the drab little dress, like a miniature virago in disguise. 'I hope I never see you again,' she said as she reached the door, stammering a little. She went out, banging the door behind her, uneasily aware that she had said almost none of the calm sensible things she had been going to say and had instead said a great many things she had never meant to say at all. All the same she was still carried high on the tide of her rage as she turned into the gateway at her home, to find the Daimler standing in old-fashioned splendour before the door. She hadn't been too sure what she was going to do next, but of one thing she was now certain, she wouldn't be able to bear Lady Belway— and what was the old lady doing at her home anyway?

She switched the engine on again with the idea of taking the car somewhere quiet for an hour or so until the old lady should be gone, but in this she was frustrated by her mother, who appeared at the drawing room window and begged her to come inside at once. Even then Augusta hesitated, but when she saw her mother turn and speak to someone inside the room, she shrugged her shoulders, got out of the car and went slowly indoors.

Lady Belway seemed pleased to see her. 'You passed us going into the village,' she observed. 'You've been to see dear Constantijn?'

Augusta took the tea her mother had poured and chose a chair with its back to the light. 'Yes. What a delightful day—you must have enjoyed your drive down, Lady Belway?' She spoke at random—anything to keep the conversation away from Constantijn.

But the old lady was not easily shaken off. 'Briggs brought the Daimler down today—I came down with Constantijn yesterday, after Susan left—and the relief...' She looked sharply at Augusta who had dropped her spoon and was taking a long time to pick it up. 'You know about that, of course.'

She was momentarily diverted while Mrs Brown proffered cake, but returned at once to the attack. 'I can't understand why you are here, Augusta. Constantijn told me that you were on duty this weekend,' she went on a little acidly. 'He talked about you for the entire journey.'

'Did he?' Augusta tried to keep the bewilderment out of her voice. 'I—I wonder why?'

Lady Belway gave a cackle of laughter. 'My dear gal, what a ridiculous question!'

Augusta remained silent, trying to think of a way of finding out exactly what Lady Belway had meant about Susan. The faint doubt that she might have been a little hasty in her conclusions crossed her worried mind. After all, Constantijn, even if he hadn't behaved quite like a man in love, hadn't appeared in the least guilty or even uneasy. She threw a speaking glance across the room to her mother, who had taken no part in the conversation, but who now responded to her daughter's look of entreaty and turned to her guest, saying persuasively:

'You know, Lady Belway, I find it all so confusing about Susan, because I had no idea... I've never met her, of course, but Augusta has told me of her, and how disturbing for Constantijn as her guardian—that she should fall in love with one of his oldest friends—a married man too. Do you suppose there's much harm done?'

Lady Belway, who had told the tale once, was only too glad to repeat herself, for it was something she would not be able to discuss outside the family, and after all the worry with dear Susan over the last few weeks, it was a relief to talk about it, and of course, since Constantijn was going to marry Augusta, she felt she might consider Mrs Brown as family—or nearly so.

'I think not—owing, I must admit, to Constantijn's handling of the whole unhappy affair. It is due to his discretion that there has been no inkling of gossip, and to his patience and good nature that Susan has come to her senses. What he said to persuade her I shall never know, nor is he likely to say what passed between himself and James—all I know is that James has gone back to that sweet wife of his and Susan has gone to Paris to stay with Huib and his wife. Constantijn is not a man to complain, but even he must have been severely tried by his trips to Cumbria, but

of course he has always had a deep regard for Mary—
James' wife, you know—and he was prepared to do
everything in his power to help her, even at the cost
of his own private affairs.' She paused for breath and
looked across at Augusta, sitting so still that she appeared not to breathe. 'I daresay you found it very
tiresome, my dear, but of course you would understand that he had his duty to his ward and his friends,
but I feel sure he made that plain.'

Augusta didn't answer this remark. She got to her
feet, banging her cup and saucer on the table in her
hurry. 'I have to go,' she said, breathless. 'Please excuse me—something—something I...' She gave both
ladies a smile of such radiance that they blinked as
she went from the room.

There was no traffic on the road this time. She
made the short trip in record time, even for her, and
brought the car to an untidy halt before Dr Soames'
front door. This time, however, she didn't go in the
surgery door but walked round the house until she
came to the french windows standing open on to the
garden. She hurried through them so clumsily that she
stumbled a little as she finally came to a halt in the
doctor's consulting room. Constantijn was standing
exactly as she had left him—she could hear the coins
still jangling in his pockets, and the sound was so
delightful that she closed her eyes for a moment with
the sheer pleasure of it, but only for a moment.

He said genially, 'Hullo, I thought you'd be back,'
and Augusta found this so unexpected that she asked
'Why?'

'My godmother is having tea with your mother; she

considers you to be—er—one of the family—a sufficiently good reason for her to confide in your mother. She has, I feel sure, told you the whole story.'

Augusta nodded, then, 'You knew I'd come back—were you so sure of me?'

He took his hands out of his pockets and stood erect, so that he seemed to tower over her. He said with tenderness, 'No, my darling heart, but I thought that if I stayed exactly where I was and thought about you, you might think of me too, for after all, you are the other half of me, are you not, dear Roly?'

She smiled a little, feeling a warm glow of happiness welling up deep inside her. 'What would you have done if I hadn't come back?'

'Come after you, of course. But it wouldn't have been quite the same.'

'No. Oh, no, Constantijn, darling Constantijn. I'm so ashamed of myself; I've been such a fool—I thought you and Susan...' She frowned. 'You might have told me...I wouldn't have blabbed it around.'

'Yes, I might. I did try, but if you remember, my darling, you were on at one, and not off until nine, and no hope of a weekend.'

She had the grace to blush. 'Oh well, I thought—but there were four days after that.'

'I had to go to Cumbria again—you know now that James and Mary live there. I took Susan there just before the dance—a desperate thing to do, but I was a desperate man.' He took a step towards her. 'I had no right to involve you—I hadn't even asked you to marry me.' He came a little nearer, smiling. 'Are you still angry?'

'Yes—no. I thought you didn't love me.' She drew an unsteady breath. 'You never said you did—not once!' she burst out.

He pulled her gently into his arms. 'I have been gravely at fault,' he remarked on a laugh. 'It shall be remedied immediately.'

It was quite some considerable time later that Augusta asked into his shoulder, 'You don't mind that I'm not beautiful?'

He put a hand under her chin and stared down at her with real astonishment. 'My dear love, you're the most beautiful woman I have ever seen or ever shall see.'

She blinked her green eyes, for she could hear by his voice that he really believed what he was saying. What was it he had once said? 'Beauty was in the eye of the beholder.' She gave a small contented sigh and arranged herself more comfortably against his shoulder, and then lifted her head once more to inquire, 'Must you really go back to Alkmaar on Monday?'

He kissed the top of her head. 'Yes, my darling, and what is worse, surgery is half an hour earlier this evening. Will you wait in the sitting room for me?— and while you're there you'd better decide what you're going to wear at our wedding, for that's all the time you're going to get.' The buzzer on the desk sounded and he took her by the shoulders and pushed her gently towards the door. 'Out of my sight, my darling Miss Brown,' he said in a voice which suggested otherwise. 'You distract my thoughts.'

Augusta walked obediently to the door. Her hand

on the handle, she paused and looked at him over her shoulder. 'I've always liked the idea of living in Alkmaar,' she said, and went out, blowing him a kiss as she went.

Harlequin Romance®

Delightful

Affectionate

Romantic

Emotional

Tender

Original

Daring

Riveting

Enchanting

Adventurous

Moving

**Harlequin Romance—the
series that has it all!**

HROM-G

HARLEQUIN 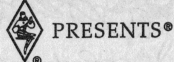 PRESENTS®

The world's bestselling romance series...
The series that brings you your favorite authors,
month after month:

Helen Bianchin...Emma Darcy
Lynne Graham...Penny Jordan
Miranda Lee...Sandra Morton
Anne Mather...Carole Mortimer
Susan Napier...Michelle Reid

and many more uniquely talented authors!

Wealthy, powerful, gorgeous men...
Women who have feelings just like your own...
The stories you love, set in exotic, glamorous locations...

HARLEQUIN PRESENTS,
Seduction and passion guaranteed!

Visit us at www.eHarlequin.com

HPGEN00

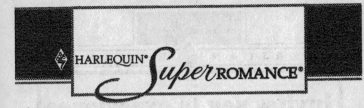

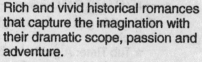